THE SOUND MIRROR

THE SOUND MIRROR

by

Heidi James

Bluemoose

Copyright © Heidi James 2020

First published in 2020 by
Bluemoose Books Ltd
25 Sackville Street
Hebden Bridge
West Yorkshire
HX7 7DJ

www.bluemoosebooks.com

British Library Cataloguing-in-Publication data
A catalogue record for this book is available from the British Library

Paperback 978-1-910422-58-8

Hardback 978-1-910422-59-5

Printed and bound in the UK by Short Run Press

It's a true image, born of a false spectacle.
Jean Genet

*What cannot be said above all must not be silenced
but written.*
Jacques Derrida

For my husband, Joe,
and our children, Talulah, Raif and Indira
(and Romi Pearl)

TAMARA

She is going to kill her mother today. But she's no monster. She's not the villain. It's a beautiful day for it, winter sharp, the sky an unfussy blue. She's taken two days holiday from work and hired a fancy car, a Mercedes, essential for this journey, where appearances and a quick getaway are everything. The man gave her a discount when she told him where she was going. The two-hundred-mile round trip will be a breeze. She's dressed carefully too: just jeans and a shirt, but they are expensive, well-cut. Understated, but a signal to those in the know. So here we are, driving down to be face to face with her for the last time. Of course, we're along for the ride. How could we not?

It's been a long time coming, and our fault, we should say. Funny that, speaking with one voice now, agreeing with each other. But yes, our fault, and all the others, tangled up with poisons and infections and rottenness. Our mothers and mothers' mothers containing us, we, in their bellies, seeds of each in the cells and the breath. Before the splitting in two, the doubling like an atomic bomb so now she holds us all, a rabble of ancestors, pressing up from inside against her skin. And she contains the next generation, too, if she wanted. If she can bear to, bear it, bear a child. Who could blame her if not? But for now, she's the sum of all us women, the total. She is what's left.

You imagine history trails you like clanging tin cans on a wedding car, but you're wrong. History is a halter that leads; we're beasts of burden with a ring through our nose. You go where we lead. We are not whole, we are fragments, un-unified, unstable entities colliding under the swirling universe. Overflowing with

1

memories and feelings not our own; archives of those who came before. It's almost romantic, imagining we're individuals, cut off from the rest, making ourselves feel special. What we are is the story she is made of. Then of course there's free will, if you believe in that, which she does. It's a nice idea anyway. That we are free to choose our actions, and the consequences.

Passive, she drifts where she's pushed, lifted and dropped. Caught in tides she can't fathom, impulses and currents she can't navigate.

She has bad dreams, always has had. Some of them are gifts from us, but not all. Sometimes she dreams of walking through the house where there are spiders as big as dinner plates, hunched wicked in the corners of the rooms, sharp as crabs. Or she dreams about running into a forest to escape something bad, but it's the forest that traps her, the branches reaching out to grab like woody tentacles. Or she dreams about floating through a void, a space of white nothing, picking up speed until she's crushed against a body covered in spikes, its face a raw grimace. Lately she dreams about a row of shoes, all the same size, neatly lined up. A pair of those slip-on garden clogs, some fluffy slippers, loafers with rubber soles, and a pair of impeccable mid-heel court shoes. They are her size but when she puts them on, they begin to shrink, crushing her toes and the bones of her foot.

There is something wrong with her, with us. Now it's down to her to purify our bloodline, obviously a blood ritual is the best way to do that. Think of the men in Sicily who at Easter scourge their sins by lashing at their flesh; the throats of livestock cut for Diwali in Nepal; the power of Kali destroying before she can create. She has to kill her, make the cut, let out the poison and end the curse. She is on the way to kill her mother, our daughter.

She is losing her hearing, but if she is honest, which she finds difficult, she quite enjoys the new deafness, the world around her muted behind her thoughts and the high-pitched ringing of tiny bells. She read that tinnitus can drive a person to suicide, but she likes it. She imagines that she is privy to the secret sounds of her body or, more romantically, the universe moving through her body.

It can't last though: people are losing patience with her, telling her to go to the doctor to get her ears checked. But she doesn't want to hear, and that's probably what aggravates them, her lack of interest in what they say.

She is listening to the ringing as she drives. There are many sounds, all pitched a tone or so differently, a chorus of ringing. Sometimes they pulse and waver; at others they are more constant, but they're all in harmony. They are echoes of our voices of course. Intrusions.

She manoeuvres the car through the traffic, edging towards the A-road that will spit her out of the city onto the motorway that skirts the suburbs and slices the shrinking countryside. Tattered Christmas decorations still sag between the street lights, the council slack in their seasonal duties. A lorry outside the butcher's sways as two men unload the pretty pale pinks and whites of hollowed-out carcasses, clean of rude, sloppy life and unrecognisable as breathing, nuzzling, shitting livestock.

She was a student when she first moved here, taking advantage of the cheap rents and distance from home. Her mother couldn't believe she'd choose to live somewhere so dirty, so dangerous, so... ethnic.

Then, the High Street was a line of charity and discount shops with lurid piles of plastic buckets and towers of multi-coloured laundry baskets piled on the pavement. There was a second-hand furniture shop whose sign boasted they cleared *all* houses, no house too big or too small; an internet café that sold Khat and wired cash overseas, a betting shop and two pubs – one for the old men and one where the younger lot bought their ecstasy and speed and only drank Coke. There were Indian, Chinese,

Turkish, African, Jamaican and pizza restaurants. Next door to the small post office that cashed dole cheques and sold a few stamps was the pawn shop, its windows filled with items too valuable to keep: guitars, jewellery, a saxophone and, once, a stuffed hippo head.

It's nothing like that now. It was nothing like that before, of course. Before, it was squatters and bombsites and old mattresses and pyramids of old fridges, and glue sniffers and drunks and militants and punks and rumours of riots. Before that, it was all salt of the earth types, ordinary: the butcher's shop, a bakers, greengrocers, haberdasher, pubs obviously; complete with a local bobby who clipped you round the ear, and other terrible things that to mention would be letting the side down. Before that, more sedate: the middle classes with their new money and nice ideas and short commute back into the city centre and mundane horrors and bored women, and before that a village, and onwards and more of the same. Backwards and forwards and always people. All the bad stuff in the past, because it's different now, isn't it? Isn't it? We know better now. Don't we? Don't you?

A slow shift of atmosphere. One fancy little coffee shop opens and, before you know it, the original tenants have been ousted till the street's almost unrecognisable and only the small convenience shop survives. The street has been colonised bit by bit, the takeover gradual. Now it's reassuringly bland, smug. They belong. They have a lifestyle. The large pub on the corner still serves pie and mash, but the mash is truffled and the pie is artisanal and crafted from hand-ground flour. Everywhere and everyone looks the same. The Pilates/yoga studio. The book/vinyl shop. Only the vape shop brings the tone down. Otherwise it all looks like an advert for a bank. Who knows where the unphotogenic people have gone? She watches a large black dog with gold eyebrows wait at the zebra crossing for a break in the traffic; it's alone, no human with it. It makes her smile.

She can feel her feet, her hands, her buttocks. She feels herself in contact with the world, with the seat, the steering wheel, the pedals. She can feel her face, she's breathing, she swallows, gulps, but she feels like she's hovering on the periphery waiting to be absorbed, accepted into her own body. Our body. It's doubling, splitting, dying, morphing, mutating. Her mother says, 'When you have a baby, when you give life, you kill yourself. Remember that.' She is ten and has asked if the hard lumps growing under her nipples are cancer. She is not sure if that means she is dying too, as she has killed her mother. The lumps grow bigger, then she bleeds. Her mother says, 'Don't cry or I'll give you something to cry for,' and hands her a pack of sanitary towels. 'Make these last, they don't grow on trees.' Her body fails her. Embarrassing. Shameful. 'Be careful not to be a slut,' her mother adds.

A deep bassline rolls through her. Dancing her, moving her. Delirium. Beats alter her metabolism, her heart rate, her breath. Dancing, longitudinal compressions merge with the MDMA, the disco biscuit she took earlier, and now every nerve is alive, the beat throbbing in her bones, her hollows, her blood. In contact with all the molecules of the universe, she moves at one with gravity, the moon, a celestial being for a few hours. The already fragile membrane containing her self dissolves. Someone smiles at her, offers her a drink from their water bottle. Everyone smiles at everyone. Her body pulses and settles. Even her liver feels joyous. It's no wonder she doesn't like sex that much. So narrow and singular in comparison. So irritating and banal. This is communion.

Her mother shakes her shoulders, flips her hands and whips her hair back and forth. The sun flickers behind the shape of her body. She grabs the child by her wrists and pulls her into a circle of skipping and hopping. The kitchen floor is cracked and cool under bare feet. Half stomp, half tip toe. Toast with jam on the eating ledge. A coffee cup. Beaker of squash. 'I love this song,' the mother breathes. A song about sugar and sexy, about touching and knowing. A man's voice, he sounds like he has swallowed grit, like he is poorly, should go to bed. Her mother lets go of her and struts across the room, her arms waving above her head, and the girl mirrors the woman, a beat behind. The mother catches the child's eye and pouts, one hand on her cocked hip. The child mimics. Eight floors up, safe in their eyrie. The mother laughs and ruffles the child's hair, as thick and dark as her own. 'Eat your breakfast now.'

'You call that music?' her mother says, her black hair razored sharp and practical around her ears. Their faces meet in the mirror. She turns off her stereo. 'They beat their women, you know.'

'Who does?'

'Men like him.' Her mother thumbs at the boy waiting for her at the bottom of the stairs.

'What do you mean?'

'No white boy will ever touch you now.'

A time slippage, opening, mixes, pockets in pockets, no distinction between the past and present, or future. The past breaks in, rips a tear in Now and intrudes. The future intervenes in here, now, a new space. Transported. The old warehouse where she went to her first raves, still illegal then, is now one of those start-up office spaces offering flexible rent for 'solopreneurs'. She's almost out of the city, picking up pace, now driving past the empty stadia, the shiny empty flats, the big shopping mall. Rows of brick terraces. Traffic lights determine her progress.

CLAIRE

Like sardines, all squashed together on the platform their names on brown labels hanging from their necks with their gas masks. Sucking fingers, thumbs, chewing nails. Catch worms doing that. Peeking over at her mum, standing with the other mothers, Maryann, the new baby, in her arms and little June at her side. They're staying at home cos they's so little and Mum won't leave Dad, anyway Mum always loves the babies best. She looks dead worried, does Mum, biting her lip and blinking a lot. Some of the other kids are scared, even crying, but Claire ain't, she ain't even holding her big sister Annie's hand. It's proper bedlam with all the crowding and the crying and the train huffing steam but a man in a uniform is walking round like he knows what he's doing; and anyway, won't it be nice to get away from the bombs, and that stinking cold shelter that lets the rain in, and that stinking siren that goes off even when she's at school and that sounds like her brother, Bert, crying when he's got a stuffed up nose. She don't like watching the dog fights, not even way up in the sky, not even the time they watched a Kraut plane get hit and the men drop out dangling under their white parachutes like unravelled yo-yos. She wants to get out of there and she's heard Wales is like Heaven, all clean and fresh air and mountains with ladies in funny tall hats.

But when they arrive in Wales, hungry and tired, and are sitting on the floor in the cold village hall waiting to be collected by their new family, she changes her mind. She don't like the strange voices and the looming hills and sheep and cows and words even she can't read. She sits close to Annie and holds Bert's sticky hand tight as the hall empties out, kid by kid. There's only a few of them left. A nice-looking lady comes, looks them over and smiles. She even shakes their hands. 'I can only take two,' she says, and there's a bit of whispering and the adults look over at her and the lady in charge of it all says, 'Never mind, you'll see each other in school, you're only down the road from each other.' And then Claire is stood there all alone with tears scratching the back of her eyes, and Annie has to carry Bert, he's that upset.

She hates Mrs Nash from the off. She hates the coat she's wearing over her apron, and the ugly hat she's pulled on over her short grey hair. She hates the way Mrs Nash looks at her like she's the last loaf in the shop. She really hates the way Mrs Nash stomps off down the road leaving her to run along behind.

When Claire catches up Mrs Nash says, 'I won't put up with any of those dirty London ways. Not in my house.' When Claire answers, 'I ain't from London,' Mrs Nash sneers and says, 'Think we're clever do we, Little Miss High and Mighty?'

The Nash's is at the end of a small terrace. The woman leads her down the side passage and leaves her in the yard. 'You'll wait there and take your things off then put them in that bucket.' When Mrs Nash comes back out she's taken off her coat and hat and is carrying a strange pair of scissors. 'Come on then, we've not got all the day.' Mrs Nash watches as Claire takes off her pullover and frock and puts them in the bucket with her coat. 'Everything,' the woman says. 'All of it.'

'No.' She ain't a baby no more but she wants her mum. She wants Annie and Bert and she wants to go home. But she ain't a baby and she's not going to let some old woman push her around. 'I'm keeping me drawers on.'

'Suit yourself, you can sleep in the shed with the other filthy animals, but I'll not have you in my house till I know you're clean. Nasty, lousy thing.'

Mr Nash is all right, though. At tea he says, 'You're small for ten, aren't you? We better feed you up,' and he puts more potatoes on her plate.

'Don't spoil her,' his wife says, 'she'll eat us out of house and home. I've already had to boil all her clothes. She was crawling alive with fleas.'

Mr Nash winks. 'Did someone mistake you for a sheep?' Claire shakes her head. Her scalp is cold and sore and, even worse, her hair was her only prettiness. 'You look like you've been shorn. Not to worry, I'll get you a nice hat to wear to school.' Yeah, he's all right that Mr Nash, even if he's a Methodist. Even so, she hates the single bed with the neat corners and the quiet that seeps into your bones with its chilly loneliness that not even the wireless can stop.

ADA

It is said, she was told, that if a pregnant woman gazed at the Himalayas and wished for a beautiful child, it would be so. But now she is far from the mountains, thousands of sea miles from her ayah, from the crumbling brick of the bungalow where spiders hang like Christmas ornaments, far from the furious heat of summer and pure wet of monsoon, peacock blue and elephant grey, dust and cow dung, the mean hunch of vultures, tea cups and pearl inlays, the smell of engine oil and burning sugar, ghee and sandalwood; closer now to the place they – or at least her father – called home. Her father and grandfather have gone on ahead, to settle into their new positions on the English railway and find them a house. They have left her mother's parents behind, at least for now, while they find the documents to prove their Britishness.

She leans on the railings, watching the gunmetal sea lift and fall. Was it that colour because of the war, from the remnants of bombs and the killing machines dissolving in the salt water? She had seen the news reels, read the papers and, although the Japanese had dropped bombs on Calcutta, she had been at school and so the war had seemed so very far away. It was only hearing Ayah crying at night when her brother didn't return from Egypt, fighting for the bloody British, that she realised it was real, not a story in a book or gossip whispered after lights out. Now they are heading for bloody Britain, she is alone for once without even Daddy to pester her, looking out to sea and wearing one of her new frocks, and a stolen smudge of lipstick.

She is the only one who hasn't got sick. The others, her mother and sister, the other wives and children from their colony, are all green at the gills and have been from the off.

The ghastly food hasn't helped, nor being on the port side of the ship. Thirty-eight days from Calcutta, pressing through the violence of the ocean, crossing the burning line of the equator and back again and now finally rounding the rock of Gibraltar towards England.

'Did you make that wish, Mummy?' she had asked, sitting on the veranda, skirt tucked around her knees, her parents drinking from tall glasses of gin and tonic.

'Yes, as a matter of fact I did, when I was pregnant with your sister.'

Her father cleared his throat.

'And not for me?'

Her mother raised the heavy lids of her dark eyes and gazed at her. 'No, we weren't anywhere near the mountains then, but never mind.' She looked away. Of course, her sister was beautiful and beloved and fragile, the poor thing, and that was why she got to stay at home and go to the local school, whilst Ada was boarded with the wretched nuns and their willow switches and leather belts. Far away from trouble and temptation: not hers, but his, but still one takes the shame and the blame with you, and the secrets.

She has left behind her piano, her pretty birds in their gilt cage, her ayah. She has left behind her books, the wild roses growing in the hedges, the scent of cumin and turmeric, indigo and pink, the puffs of laundry steam stiff with starch, the flat breads and servants chatter, anger and white cloth, the riots and fury, the children shitting and playing and sleeping in the streets, the thrum of the spinning jenny and the charkha and the old unbelonging; of being kutcha butcha, half-baked bread, neither British nor Indian. They have left behind them the railways and the Institute with its dances and tea parties, cricket on the maidan, picnics with the Simmonds and the Da Silvas and the others from the compound. They have left the crowds shouting *Go home! Go home!* Neighbours turning on one another, massacres and a new country torn from the

TAMARA

It's about time she finished her mother off. She's given it a couple of goes – if you count her birth, then the exhaust pipe shenanigans. She almost succeeded when she was fifteen: her face new-minted with a black eye, fat jaw, loose teeth, and this time hitting back and hitting hard and finding herself straddling her mother with her hands ringing her neck. Wringing it too. Ha! That was just after Christmas as well. You have to laugh or you'll die crying.

Would you believe she's made something of herself? Has a lot to lose. Owns her flat, which has a balcony and a fitted kitchen. Pot plants. She has a degree. She is the head of communications for a bank. She has her own office, outside of which her team of four sits. It isn't a very large team, but still... She is very good at her job. She knows how to please, what people need to hear, want to hear, must hear. She is on message. Protector of the brand. Flim flam. Sham. So what, she makes money, relies on no one.

She wasn't alone at Christmas. She had dinner with friends – Pav and Toby, Sara and Harriet, Gio and Aisling. She wore an Alexander McQueen cashmere jumper in blue with Kooples trousers. She arrived with tasteful gifts from Liberty and brought champagne and Rococo chocolates. She is not a failure. Her photo of the meal got eighty likes on Instagram.

But still she doesn't fit in. She reads the books everyone loves, buys the clothes, follows the people she wants to emulate on social media, spends hours going through magazines and on Pinterest and Instagram looking at what other women are wearing, doing, eating, being. She doesn't really know who she is. Even at her age. Which is thirty-something. She googles 'What is a good life?' and 'How to live well' and 'What is the meaning of life?' It never gives a satisfactory answer.

She embarrasses herself, as confused as a moody teenager. Perhaps it's because she is out of time, anachronistic; she suffers from a nostalgia for a world she wasn't born in but was taught to hang on to. Raised in part by her grandparents and mostly by books, she half exists in the world conjured by Noel Streatfeild and Enid Blyton: cycling to unshadowed woods, dining in wood-panelled rooms, silences broken by bird song not super woofers. Ticking clocks and elevenses and tea cakes. None of this is a world she could have inherited from anywhere but what she read and wanting to be somewhere else, somewhere far from free school dinners, second-hand school uniform, coats piled on the bed in winter and only one pair of shoes.

Still, she hates it: no matter how hard she tries or how much she spends, she doesn't belong, she's always too late. It's exhausting. She should give up, but she keeps trying and then hates everyone else for being what they are. Comfortable. Hates herself more, of course. Is ashamed of herself. As a consequence she doesn't look anyone in the eye, seems shady, sly. She feels that she has something to hide, something sick and dirty. That she isn't good enough, not wanted. At risk. But it's we that should be ashamed. Or should we?

Did your mother leave you in the woods, like Hansel and Gretel? Did she trap you in a tower with only a window and your skein of hair? Like all fairy tales, there's always a bad or dead mother. It's no secret, it's hardly new. Blame the mother. It's her fault. Our fault. We're used to it. Broad shoulders can take the load. As a baby she is left out in the garden between feeds. Tucked in her pram like one of Harlow's little monkeys. An experiment. She is fed every four hours on the dot. She has already learnt not to cry, as Mother is ignoring her. She must not be spoilt:

spoiling a baby makes a rod for your own back. The baby is enraged with the mother. The baby craves the mother.

She wakes in the night and her mother has gone. She is not a baby any more. She is too big for nappies and gets a slap on the bottom to teach her to be clean. The mother has taken her to live in a flat far away from her grandparents and their overcrowded, noisy house. Her mother isn't in her bed, nor listening to records curled up on the gold velour sofa she's bought on tick, she isn't on the balcony smoking a fag, she isn't in the toilet. The child is alone. She tries to phone Nanna, but doesn't know anything about dialling a number, only that when she is handed the receiver, Nanna or Grandad's voice is there, wafting like smoke into her ear. The dial tone hums its dead note. They are not there. She is alone. She is going to die. Bad things happen to little children left alone.

She is caught in the blind squeeze of panic. She runs to the front door, shut firm. She looks around the flat again. Toilet, Mummy's bedroom, her bedroom, living room, kitchen. Looks under the beds. Pulls open the airing cupboard in the hallway. She hopes this is a terrible game of hide and seek. She can't find her. She is crying. Gulping, hiccupping, snot, salt tears. She drags the kitchen chair down the corridor to the front door and climbs up carefully. On tip toes to reach the handle. Twisting the knob, slipping in her wet hands but the door pulls open, only a crack because the chair is blocking its path. She pulls and pulls, too young, too panicked to get down from the chair and move it. Too panicked to know what to do. Too little to understand leaving the flat would be more dangerous anyway.

She calls through the gap between door and jamb, 'Lady, lady next door, my mummy has gone. Lady, help.' Perhaps she only calls once or twice, perhaps she is screaming. She is screaming. Her head hurts. She wees herself, but only a little. The lady next door doesn't come, but the mother does, eventually, appearing in the doorway like magic. The mother lifts the child in her arms and puts her back to bed.

CLAIRE

She don't half love Samson, his whiskers and fat lips that reach like fingers for a carrot. She loves the wiry black hair of his mane and the white soft fur under his belly that's round like the stove. Her favourite job, looking after him: mucking him out, feeding him his mash, cleaning his harness and rubbing the wax into the leather to keep it soft so it don't rub him as he works. Just being near him, all warm and safe. He's her pal, and he likes her, likes her better than Annie. Annie said he stood on her foot on purpose, and that Claire can look after the stinking nag for all she cares, but Claire knows he wouldn't stand on no foot, not on purpose, he's as dainty as a wren for such a lump. Annie likely pinched him or pulled his tail. That would be just like her, spiteful moo. Samson likes Claire even better than Dad, he told her so: he said, 'You've got a way with that animal' and she couldn't wipe the grin off her face. It was Samson she missed the most and Samson she was happiest to see when they got back from Wales. Now she misses the clean bed and quiet room and the books Mr Nash give her to read and the dinners and tinned peaches and evaporated milk that the missus give her, even though she had a face like a slapped arse. Not even a year they was gone for, but funny how you start belonging some place, how what felt strange becomes ordinary and what was ordinary is strange and you don't belong anywhere any more or to no one neither.

She finishes picking out the stones and muck in his feet and checking his shoes are fixed tight when Bert sticks his head around the door.

'You nearly done in here? Mum wants you.'

'All right, I'm coming.'

'Hurry up then.'

'I said all right, didn't I?'

She runs her hand down Samson's neck and presses her face against his cheek, his head resting on her shoulder. 'Night boy,' she tells him and bolts the stall door. She crosses the yard, her boots grinding against the cement, past Dad's cart loaded up for tomorrow and covered up for the night, ducking under the lines of washing still out and into the house.

Her mother sits on the armchair next to the stove, her head tipped back, the gold crucifix around her neck moving up and down as she breathes; her only other jewellery is her wedding ring, and her finger swells around it like proving bread. She's a bit like Samson, with her round belly, her long black hair and ankles as thick as his hocks. They was only away a year, but mum has got another baby coming. Always babies coming, more mouths to feed, more hard work. Blessings from God that Mrs Nash said, easy for her to say who had none of her own and just as well an' all, cos look how nasty she was. Her mum looks done in, so many kids she can hardly remember their names, let alone have room to love 'em all, only the newest one. She loves 'em and then when they get big, the older ones get 'em and the love has worn out.

'What's up, Mamma?'

Without lifting her head or looking at her she says, 'Go help Annie put the little ones to bed.' Her voice has still got the whiff of wop about it, that's what Bert says, and it don't do to hang on to all that old country stuff; Dad got collared by the police for being a wop. They thought he was a spy or on Hitler's side or something silly. They's all English now, ain't they? Born here and everything.

'Yes Mamma,' she says, because she does try to be a good girl and she don't want the belt and she even loves her really, even if she ain't half embarrassed by her. 'Where's Dad?'

'Gone for the midwife, this one is coming. Go help your sister, yes?'

As she goes she hears her mother cry out like a little 'un for her own mamma, but she's back in the village on the island a long way away, so it's a waste of her breath.

She peeks in the crib at the new baby. It's a boy. She has three sisters and now two brothers. There's been others, but no one mentions the dead ones. She picks up Maryann to let her see the baby, but Maryann struggles, not wanting to be lumped about like a sack of spuds. Claire dumps her down on the floor so she can play with her raggy doll. She's to watch the little ones, but all she wants to do is read her book or play out with Dotty from up the road. Fat chance of that, all her mum does is rest and sleep and cry. This time it's a worry cos her milk ain't come in, but Dad says she's never failed him yet. Mrs Butler from next door's been round, clucking over the baby and smiling at her mum, though Claire has heard her and the nasty old girl in the butchers talk about her, saying how those Italians breed like rabbits, bloody Catholics as bad as the Irish, worse, cos they don't even speak the language and who knows what side they're on, might be living here but they're the enemy now. Bloody old cow. Annie is boiling up milk from the scheme and giving it to the baby in a bottle, but he still looks grey, tiny, like a doll dug out of the rubble.

She rolls her tongue over the sweet tucked between her jaw and her cheek, bright orange and aniseed. She's been trying not to crunch it up ever since Dad came home and shared them out between them all to celebrate the new baby. Mum said the baby's name was Giovanni, but Dad weren't having none of it and said we'll call him George. A good English name. So George it is.

She wipes the snot off Maryann's face and pushes the door open a crack on her mum and dad's bedroom. The curtains are pulled, but a ruler of light marks out the heap her mum makes on the bed. The room smells stale, ripe, like the sawdust on the butcher's floor. 'Mamma,' she whispers, but the heap don't move. She wonders why she lets it happen. Annie says mum knows the old ways, the tricks to bring her blood on, but it's a sin and Dad would give her a wallop and tell her she's unnatural, just like the time once before, and so she just keeps on. More babies, her thick black hair getting straggly and thin and her daughters doing the raising up, dragging up more like. How would he know though? If she just sorted it out before it proper took? What business is it of his anyway? He ain't the one carrying it, back bending, thickening, heavy as a barge. He ain't the one pushing it out into the world, feeding and mopping up, wearying away and trying to find enough love. Cos she's not even a mum herself and yet it's like she's always known how, a dab hand with a little one before she even knew how they was got and already she's bloody tired of it.

What she loves best, almost as much as Samson, is school, now that it's back on, and Miss Butler, because if she does all her letters and arithmetic and sits still and polite at her desk then she's allowed to choose a book. The other girls laugh at her, staying inside and reading and reading, but she's no teacher's pet, and so what anyway? Who cares what they think? Stupid mares. She loves the words that make pictures in her mind and the way a story makes sense and tricks along like a journey made easy by good grub and a song. She loves how she can slow it down and speed it up, how she can go back a page or two and re-read the best bits, the bits that make her laugh so hard she wants to wet herself. Then she wins a prize for handwriting, a bar of chocolate and a lovely book about Alice in Wonderland. She's so happy she could burst and she runs home to show 'em the book and tells them how Miss Butler said her cursive writing was a beautiful thing to behold and her mum smiles and tries to quiet little George, who's forever fussing and crying and Dad says, 'Careful, Claire, pride comes before a fall.' So she takes her book and puts it by the bed she shares with Annie, June and Maryanne and is glad she ate all the chocolate on the way home, even if she does feel sick, because she is bloody fed up of sharing all the time. And she keeps a secret, even though secrets are hard to keep in this house all nosy beggars, but her secret is that Miss Butler says she's doing so well she might even get the scholarship and get to go to the Grammar school.

It starts with shivers, too hot, too cold. Teeth clattering. Her head banging like the clappers. Too poorly for school, too poorly to do her chores, too poorly even to read a book. Her legs wobbly as a foal's. Her neck swelling up. She's put to bed in her mum and dad's room, baby George in his crib beside her, he's poorly with it too, so poorly he don't even cry. Mamma has pulled the curtains for 'em, only the dark will do. No one else is allowed in, and even though she drifts in and out of a sticky, murky sleep she feels mamma there, wiping her face with a cold cloth, holding her hand, singing soft songs in her old language, and praying over 'em, begging the Madonna for her help and Claire is happy; she would like to stay like this, sick, babied, her mother loving her. The doctor comes, a long man leaning over her brother first, shaking his head, then her, looking in her mouth and listening to the thump of her chest. He gives her mother a brown bottle of medicine and tells her what to do, his voice stretched thin.

'Why did you wait so long to call?' he asks as he packs away his things.

Her mother shakes her head the way she does when she is unsure and her tongue is stuck. Later Dad shouts about the cost of calling the doctor, about letting nature take its course, about mouths to feed and being bled dry. She hears Annie and Bert on the stairs, their mother shushing them. At night her mother takes George from his crib and gets onto the bed with Claire and rocks them both to sleep, Dad is sleeping in his armchair. Then the fever breaks, and she begins to get better little by little and her mamma lets her sit in the parlour with a blanket on her knees, listening to the wireless sometimes, or reading. She sips Bovril and gets a bit steadier on her feet. She's sent back to bed with her sisters and Mamma doesn't sponge her face any more or smooth her hair back from her face. She tells Mamma that her tummy hurts, that her head hurts, she even tries to cry, but Mamma doesn't listen because George isn't getting better. Baby George doesn't get better, and when he doesn't wake up one morning, her mother looks at her as if her getting better stole her brother's chance. No one says it, but she knows they all wished it had been her instead.

TAMARA

She keeps to the slow lane as much as she can, and takes the longest route to avoid the Dartford crossing. She is avoiding danger, for now. She is afraid that she won't be able to stop herself driving off the bridge. Her body is already braced for impact even thinking about it. She is terrified. She goes the long way round, skirting the southern borders of Hertfordshire, Surrey and Sussex before coming back to Kent. Adds almost two hours to the journey, the queue for Heathrow always a spanner in the works. London a fat spider in the centre of a tarmac web.

This one is careful, makes lists of things to do, to worry about, to complete. Not like her mother. She was impetuous, wild. She liked to get drunk and dance on tables. Naughty girl. Fast. Once she ran away with a band and was the lover of a pop star. Before our son, the father. She ran naked into the sea for a dare and made jokes and laughed at the TV and at people who fell over in the snow. Whereas this one doesn't think it's funny when people hurt themselves. This one cares what other people think of her. This one thinks carefully before she speaks, before she acts. She could be pretty if she smiled. Her mother was pretty. We were pretty, so very pretty. Well, some of us were.

We pass the occasional sign for Brexit left fading on fencing along the motorway; herds of cows graze in slow formations, so it can't rain today. She turns on the radio: politicians and journalists talk in circles, still. She switches it off. If she had a magic wish what would we undo? Seventy-odd miles to go. Not long now. She's tempted to turn back, to forget the whole thing. But she can't. We've already come too far.

Traffic slows, a jam. The woman in the passenger seat in the car next to us yawns. She is well dressed, wearing a silky cream blouse, and her make up is immaculate with long eyelashes and glossy lips. Her husband, or the man next to her whatever he is, reaches over and strokes her thigh; she smiles at him. Our girl looks away, embarrassed by the happy people separated from us by a thin sheet of metal and glass. We are so close she could touch them. Her shame and loneliness swallow her whole.

She walked in on her mother and one of her boyfriends once. She could hear the most peculiar noises, as if her mother was being hurt, so the little girl had to check she was all right. Her mother was on top of the man, her breasts exposed, her long dark hair falling over her face. Her bedside lamp was on, her pink silk scarf draped over it. It made the room a pretty colour. They didn't see the child, but he was still there when she went in for her morning cuddle, his hairy bottom hanging out of the blue covers, his arm pinning her mother down. The child was hungry and they stayed in bed for a long time, so she ate the half tin of cold baked beans she found in the fridge and waited for her mother to wake up. Their clothes were in a pile on the living room floor, next to her colouring books and the ashtray filled with cigarette butts. They took a long time.

She tells herself that her mother was entitled to her freedom, to a little love, that she shouldn't have begrudged her and when they went, the boyfriends, she was her mother's sunshine again. The moon and the stars again. But it was hard not to be jealous, not to resent them with their chunky teeth and smells, and loud voices. Their big feet and long bodies. Heavy hands and nasty fingers. Hard not to sulk, to turn away with her arms crossed hiding furious little fists and wishing them away. After the men had gone, she would comb her mother's beautiful black hair while she cried and smoked for a while, then they'd carry on. Besides, it was never as simple as a child's jealousy. At least one of her mother's lovers was less than kind, less than decent, less than human. So there it is.

The traffic moves on, slowly, she shifts into gear and the car next to us, with the elegant woman, speeds off, out of view. It's important to remember that our girl is not a monster. Neither are we, which is a miracle, all things considered.

Overhead, large birds turn and glide on the upward draughts of air. Red kites we think. She tries not to watch them and keep her eyes on the road. She'd rather watch the birds.

We're all gamblers, holding out for a change in our luck. Staying in the miserable city just a little while longer, chasing stupid dreams; voting as if we're already rich and need a tax haven; believing we can change the one we love; that happiness is being skinny; that we won't get old and infirm; putting everything, all we've got, on a future already extinct. This one always hoped that if she was good enough, if she did all her mother asked of her, she would be loved. She would be enough. She is still trying. On a hiding to nothing. Gamblers, every one of us, betting our happiness on long odds, because the real prize is too banal. Unthinkable.

For example, being top of the class, with a reading age of twelve when you are only seven, is good. Passing your Eleven Plus with the highest marks in the county is great. Using words like 'atavistic' or 'somnolent' when other, simpler words would do is going too far. Is, in fact, showing off. Worse is correcting someone on their own opinion to which they are entitled. Even worse is telling them they are a bigot, unthinking. Dense. You would do well to remember, Lady Muck, that pride comes before a fall. Who'd you think you are, anyway? Little Miss High and Mighty. You can play a winning hand too far. The house always wins. Mother is always right.

ADA

The derzi unrolls bolts of cotton, dimity and a marigold-coloured damask across the dining room table. He steps back to allow Ada and her mother to touch the fabrics, to hold them up to their faces and drape them across their shoulders. They've used the same tailor for years and, as always, his shirt and churidars are a dazzling white, his moustache a neat curl under his nose. She wonders how he stays so pristine. The only change is that now he returns Ada's smile with a frown, though that's not so unusual these days: lots of their old friends act like strangers now, or have just stopped visiting or working for them. It is as if they have done something unspeakable and have been banished from sight and no one will tell her why; Mummy didn't pin her hopes on the derzi even coming, so she should be thankful he's here at all. He watches them closely, as if they are not to be trusted.

'I rather like this pink, Mummy.'

Her mother looks up from a pale blue cotton and appraises her, her left eyebrow raised. Her nostrils flare. People say her mother would be quite pretty if she were just a little paler, and perhaps a little less brittle. 'No, it isn't flattering. That would look much better on Lilian.'

Ada thinks those people might be right. Her mother subsists on only black tea and fruit until dinner, alongside a few measly pats on the hand, and as a consequence rarely raises a smile.

'Then might I at least have something in the damask?' She holds the shimmering yellow against her cheek and imagines herself in a gold evening gown surrounded by admirers.

'Why not.'

'Oh thank you, Mummy.' She pulls a fold of paper from her pocket and carefully straightens it to show the derzi. Torn from a fashion magazine left at the Institute, the model poses in a strapless gown, her shoulders bare, a full skirt billowing from her waist all the way to the floor. 'Could you make this?'

He nods, barely concealing his contempt. 'Yes, Memsahib.'

'Let me see.' Her mother reaches out for the page. 'It's a little much, isn't it?'

'Oh please, I'm almost sixteen and Daddy said I need a formal gown for the ship.'

Her mother frowns, studies the image again. 'Then if that's what your father said, that's what we'll have. We'll take three of those please. One for both my daughters and one for me. You do have Lilian's measurements, haven't you?' The derzi nods. 'She's hardly changed, not like this one.'

'But Mummy!'

'You don't want it?' Her mother tightens her grip on the page, threatening to crush the beautiful girl in the gown.

'Yes, yes I do.' Ada balls her hands into fists and crams them into her pockets.

'Well then.' Her mother hands the paper to the derzi and begins to flick through his book of patterns, stopping to point at various garments every few pages. 'We'll need some of these skirts, blouses, a coat each. Perhaps in this, this and this.' She moves rolls of fabrics to one side of the table. The derzi writes in his note book. 'She will also need one of these.' She points at a tailored jacket and skirt suit. 'In a wool tweed, I believe.'

'But why must I have one of those? It's horrible.'

'Because it's very smart.'

The derzi has unrolled his measuring tape and, pinching it between thumb and forefinger, holds it against her particulars: waist, bust, hips, height. The air is very still; the punkah hangs vertical like a stopped pendulum. There is no one left to work the pulley.

'But it looks like a uniform, like I'm pretending to be someone else.'

He presses hard against the small of her back, making her stand straight.

'Must you always be so difficult? Your clothes speak for you, you know that. You're not a schoolgirl any more. When we get to England you're to go to secretarial school and you'll need the right outfit.' Her mother grips the back of a chair, as though she needs its support to give her strength.

'But why? I don't want to. Why can't I go to a school?'

'Don't be silly. You've passed your Senior Cambridge Level.'

'Perhaps I could go to university.'

'Why would you do that? A girl like you, what would be the point? Besides, your father says things are different there.'

'How does he know? He's never even been.'

'But your grandfather was born there, so that is how he knows.'

'Yes, but things change, Mummy.'

'Enough! You will be quiet and do as you are told. You are too much girl, that is your trouble. I see what you are, don't think that I am ignorant. Now, I have to talk to Cook about dinner and see to your poor sister. Come.' Her mother nods to the derzi, opens the French doors and goes out onto the verandah, leaving him to gather his materials and Ada to follow in her wake.

Tamara

She picks up her rucksack from the carousel. The heat moulds itself around her body, presses against her t-shirt and shorts, between the straps of her sandals. Shouldering her pack, she looks confident, at ease with these new surroundings: the boil and hum of voices she can't understand; the bright colours; the circulating smell of bodies, tooth decay, flowers and burnt sugar. But it's a trick of good posture enforced by the weight of the bag. She leaves the airport and finds a bus heading into the city centre. Squashed against the window she looks out at the traffic, the high-rise offices, the hotel towers of glass and metal, the building sites of churning cement and steel girders and billboards advertising McDonalds and Pepsi Cola. Disappointment coats her tongue. She has put off university for a year and worked on the check-out at Tesco for months to come here.

She finds somewhere to stay – a tiny single room in a cheap guest house with thin partition walls and shared toilet and shower room – and holds back silly tears. Wishing she'd listened to her mother and not come. Of course she'll be murdered or raped or both. Or worse. She wonders what would be worse than being raped and murdered. Being raped and cut into small pieces before dying? Having your eyeballs plucked out?

She pulls herself together. Tells herself she is a traveller, not a tourist. She is intrepid, she is an adventurer. She's one of us, after all, some of us travelled so far. Some of us walked and sailed and ran. Some of us stood still, holding everything up. Learning new languages, new gods, new regimes. Never looking back.

She goes on the careful walks directed by her guidebook. She looks at the temples and gold Buddhas. Boys who look like lovely girls. Who are girls as far as she can tell. She visits a floating market, where rubbish chokes the water between the narrow canoes full of fruit and vegetables, plastic toys, cooking pots, cartons of cigarettes and piles of umbrellas. Wide-brimmed hats shade the sellers' faces. She eats sticky rice with strange curries, avoids the barbecued crickets and grubs, the chicken feet and pig tails. Dodges traffic, chokes on the polluted air. Smiles until her face hurts and presses her hands together like a prayer. Does not lick the back of stamps or step on coins. She remembers not to point the soles of her feet at anyone or pat small children on the head. She rides in a tuk-tuk. Tries not to die. Politely takes photos. The neon nights she spends browsing in a shop full of used books, the owner an old white man with missing teeth and a cigarette always on the go. Occasionally she sits on a plastic chair at the plastic table of a street café and eats noodles while she watches people line up to get into the Ping Pong show opposite.

After a week or so she has exhausted the suggestions in the book and begins to wonder how she will last for three months. Disappointment in the city is replaced by disappointment in herself. She is boring. A nothing. Who was she kidding? Then the man in the bookshop, who's American and called Vince by the way, perhaps taking pity, perhaps sick of the sight of her mooning around, points out the bus to the coast and sells her a paperback copy of Zen and the Art of Motorcycle Maintenance and wishes her luck and reminds her to smile more.

At the beach she reads, gets sunburnt, and eats bananas to save money. She stays in a beach hut, watching for snakes in the shower, spiders in the bed. A group of boys, blonde and broad-shouldered arrive. They're staying in some of the huts close by. They swim and smoke weed and drink local beer and laugh. She watches, envious of how comfortable they are in their skin; even swimming, as if they belong as much in water as air and the sea doesn't burn and sting their eyes. They talk and laugh and shout. They sleep out in the open, dozing on towels with one arm slung over their eyes. Girls join them. They all move as if on wheels, or as if they're floating. At ease. At one with the machine.

One of the girls smiles at her. Asks her name, offers a beer. They tell her to bring her stuff over and hang out with them. She does. She drinks the beer, smokes the weed. And the next day. Then the next. She goes with them when they head to an island. They cross a border and then cross back. Climb up hills thick with dense green leaves. Damp. Insects the size of mice. Bats the size of rabbits. They leave offerings in temples and give cigarettes to teenage monks in orange robes. She rides on the back of motorbike, her arms loose around a naked waist. Dances under a full moon, drinks whiskey and swallows mushrooms. Sees the moon become a skull, then a bird that preens its feathers. Sleeps with Jennifer and then Brody. Then Liam. Gets a tattoo on her ankle that her mother will hate but hardly anyone will ever see. Forgets to phone her mother or remembers and doesn't bother – too far away to care, or remembers and can't find a phone that works, or can't afford it. She is still too ordinary to see something exquisite in squalor. She is a romantic, conventional. She watches the others closely and copies what they do, tries out different ways of being herself until it almost feels natural. They swim in pools fed by waterfalls. Listen to rain thump against corrugated iron. She wears tiny shorts and no one seems to agree with her mother that she has the legs of a fifty year old woman. No one seems to be disgusted by her appearance.

She misses her cheap, non-refundable flight. Calls her mother from the airport: 'Please, I'm stuck. My visa is running out. I've got no money. I know I'm stupid. I'm sorry. I'm really sorry. Please.'

Her mother listens in silence, saying only: 'You're on your own. You made your bed, now lie in it.'

CLAIRE

Missed the boat for the grammar school, the fever boiling away more than just her baby brother. But it's as worth crying over as spilt milk, because when she told Dad about the exam for the scholarship he give her short shrift. There ain't none of that nonsense, not in this house. That's what he said. Not in my house. You'll do what your sister's done and work for me. Who d'you think you are? Lady Muck? Grammar school my arse. Who'll feed you? Who'll buy the uniform? You ain't got the sense you were born with, you. I'll give you what for, so help me I will. His fist's too lazy for a proper clump though.

So she goes out on the rounds with Samson, leading him along Dad's route up and down the streets, the cart getting lighter as they go, Samson picking up to a trot past the bomb sites, tugging her past poor old Mrs Gent's house, her and her kids still stopping with the charity, her old man crushed under the rubble, and even though they'd dug him out she couldn't help shudder as if he were still under there, or at least bits of him, a hand maybe, or a toe. Houses sawn in half like magicians' ladies, door frames open to air, peeling wallpaper on single walls, one with a picture frame still hanging twenty feet up. Not just the houses are scarred and torn and ragged: there's all the men come home, but it's more than them, there's Lucy who was born with a top lip that looks ripped apart who you can barely make out what she says so end up nodding and smiling and agreeing to god knows what, old men trussed up to hold in their gut snouting through stomach walls, women whose private parts collapse from under them from the exhaustion of all them kids. It's everywhere, bodies abscessed and veined and

32

bulging and gaping and leaning and weeping. Like everyone and everything is falling apart.

Stopping for her regulars who come out with their baskets for their tatties and cabbage, apples and plums, though it changes with the season, and stopping here and there when they're called on the off chance, she sneaks Samson a carrot, or a bruised apple. It's not so bad, especially now she's knitted herself some fingerless gloves and a matching scarf so she's not as cold, and it's better than being in the shop with her dad and Annie who thinks she's proper special now she's got her monthlies and wobbly boobs, her bum fat as a cow's. She'll be courting soon and then she'll really think she's the bee's knees and be even more a pain in the backside.

At least out here it's just her and Samson, dodging the pot holes and rowdy kids, chatting with the housewives and the old people. No standing in the ration queue. She don't half miss her books and lessons though, and she ain't half tired and her feet and back ache something rotten, but the gossip and stories she hears are just as good as a book if you listen proper, and she likes learning all about the fruit and the veg, which apples are sweetest, the best eaters, best cookers. The ones that winter well and the ones that dry and shrivel like a priest's arse. How to grow 'em, bring 'em on and graft 'em and protect 'em. She likes the clean, rainy smell of the earth still crusted on the new potatoes. She loves the colours and textures, the green cucumbers, the piles of yellow potatoes and reds of cherries, the seasons that bring new shapes and colours. Not as good as home her dad says, all paler, smaller, wintery and tired here. But here is better for other reasons, so he says; he's been here so long he's lost his accent and loves it so much he wants to be English, even changing his last name. Even so, she loved her book learning and just think: she could've been an office girl, maybe even a secretary, and worn a nice skirt and blouse, stockings even. She could've had nice hands and nails. Too late now, and it don't do to have ideas above your station.

TAMARA

She isn't a whole self. She's a recording, a medium the past speaks through. She hears our voices passing through her. Ventriloquism. Our dummy. Not exactly split in two, but more than one.

Did you know that a female is born with all the eggs she will ever produce in her ovaries, and that those eggs developed when she was in her mother's womb, and that the quality of her mother's health and care in pregnancy will affect not only the baby she carries, but all the little egg cells in the child too? So we could say our grandmothers were pregnant with us too. Or pregnant with our potential. As was her grandmother, and hers and onwards and forever. No wonder the Russian matryoshka dolls seem so right. It's not the same for mothers of boys, as semen is continuously produced starting at puberty, so around thirteen or so, and doesn't end until they die. Our fathers pass on their genes, but we weren't present in our paternal grandmother's body. She did not hold our first cell inside her body, only the treasured son, he does not need to share her body with anyone, not even his own future. He alone is cherished. Maybe that's why she was able to deny our girl's existence so easily? The connection is as weak as spit.

When she is fourteen she meets her father and his family for the first time. Her grandparents, aunt, cousins, stepmother, siblings. They have always existed but only now do they exist for her. They are eerily familiar strangers. This new family exclaims over her similarities to them – her tombstone teeth, chunky limbs, high cheekbones – as if they are convincing themselves that she is really one of them. She is awkward in her sudden curves, her teenage body strange and very female. They scrutinise her, especially the grandmother, who tells her she may call her granny, and corrects her pronunciation of certain words. She sits on the edge of the floral-patterned sofa, answering their questions but mostly listening to them gift her with their life stories. She is a new audience member for them to play out versions of themselves. They tell her she was never not wanted, that her family – the mother's side – will have lied to her, whatever they've said. They have always *cared*, just from a polite distance. It was what your mother wanted, they say. She made this happen. Tamara doesn't ask why they didn't try harder to see her, or if it's true they paid her father's friends to say they'd all slept with her mother so who could prove paternity? She doesn't believe they will tell her the truth any more than her mother. We've always had a habit of not letting truth get in the way of self-preservation.

They quickly lose interest in her. Move on to new topics of conversation. She is expected to just fit in, get on with it. She learns that she is not special. Not worth listening to. She learns she must speak differently, lose weight, that she needs to unlearn everything her other family ever taught her. She learns that blood isn't thicker than water.

Her mother says, you are very difficult to love. Her mother says, you have ruined my life. You'll be the death of me, you will. She also says, I wish you had died instead, and no one wanted you except me, I fought to keep you and look at how you repay me, the only person who tried to love you. But Tamara has been loved. Christopher loved her. Until he couldn't. Until she made him stop. But the point we're making is that she has been loved.

In the beginning, Christopher asks lots of questions which she can't answer, his fingers delicately touching hers, testing her reactions, the pale length of him, over six feet tall and romantically stooped at the shoulder, his head cocked to one side as if always ready to listen. Together they make up new selves for each other's approval. Allies and custodians. He plays the only Bob Dylan song he knows on guitar and when she sings along he shakes his head. He shows her how to make poached eggs properly; though she can't taste the difference she doesn't say anything.

The pale length of him, unfurled like rope across her bed. Listening to music, music he thinks she ought to listen to as her music tastes are dull and unsophisticated, too mainstream, in his opinion. Stroking her with his girlish hand heavy on her breast, fingers quick on her expectant skin. He's remembered mainly as sensation – colour, taste and the drowsy scent of his short brown hair. Long kisses, her lips closed over the darkness. They take walks, cutting through the ancient woods at the edge of the city, hand in hand, stumbling over tree roots like lost children in a fairy tale, the swaying branches overhead shifting the shadows. He points out plants, names the birds from their calls, identifies trees. She doesn't bother to correct him: no one likes a know-it-all. She does tell him that she'd like to meet a bear in the wild.

'What if it attacked and killed you?' he asks, his narrow head cocked to one side, examining her. She shrugs, doesn't tell him that she would consider death by wild animal an act of worship. She's learnt to hide her weird.

The warning voices in her head? She ignores us. Marries him anyway. He ticks lots of good boxes. He cooks and she washes and dries. He jokes and she laughs. He gives her head, she almost orgasms; he hoovers, she dusts; he has a job, so does she. It is nice to be loved. Even her mother likes him, though the wedding is a disappointment. The dress especially, and the catering and the invites (too modern, too minimal, pretentious) but... she likes him. Her friends, especially Pav, don't like him, but they say nothing. The husband and mother joke together about her clumsiness, her forgetfulness, always with her nose in a book but somehow still so dumb. They raise eyebrows at each other when she speaks and comment on her terrible decorating skills when she paints the kitchen, the portion sizes of the meals she makes them and her lack of dexterity in ironing shirts. Her mother says she has always been cack-handed, always been useless.

Eventually when she tells him to stop taking sides with her mother, she is trembling with something. Fury? Fear?

He says, 'What has got into you?'

And she says, 'Why do you gang up on me with her?'

And he laughs and shakes his head and the laugh peters out to an exhausted sigh. 'You're too sensitive. You know it's just a laugh, we're just kidding around.'

'Well I don't like it, I want you to stop. Please.'

'You know you're paranoid and you take yourself too seriously. It's not always about you.'

'I'm not paranoid. You don't know my mother like. I do, I know what she's doing.'

'What is she doing?'

'She makes me feel small. Can't you see she is constantly criticising me and you join in?'

'Well, firstly, no one can *make* you feel anything. You allow those feelings, and secondly, no, I can't see her criticising you. I see you making no sense right now and blaming everyone else for your neurosis. She's your mother. It's sick to hate your own mother.'

'I'm not sick, and I don't hate her. You just don't understand.' She can barely breathe now, this is too much effort, like running up a mountain, or trying to remember a dream you had two nights ago. She is lost in a strange territory. Her hands and feet are numb.

'Help me to understand. And you do hate her, even if you won't say it.'

'I don't remember. I've just always felt like this. I don't remember when I started to or why. Just that since I was little I, I just, I don't know.'

He shrugs, raises a splayed hand, palm up, then lets it drop to underline his exasperation. 'Just let it go,' he says. 'Stop letting your past ruin our future, right now. It's ruining every day, our life... now. You ruin it with this obsession, this morbid... paranoia. Move on.'

He would've kept on loving her if she'd let him. He is very clear about that.

It's not all our fault. We've produced others, others who are ordinary, even happy. She has happy cousins, gay, straight, married or not. It's possible it isn't all down to us.

ADA

She is in the garden, sitting on the old rattan chair, her bare feet tucked up under her. The gardener has placed a parasol over her, to protect her from the sun. She is painting a bird with her water colours: a bright yellow breast, green wings with a turquoise flash, a black mask over the eyes. A gang of starlings tap at the soil as the sweeper moves back and forth across the terrace with a broom. The gardener is pruning the roses, tidying the beds. It's a war of attrition, it seems: an endless cutting back, plucking out weeds, unwanted plants that have the temerity to grow where the seed lands. Grass that must be mowed, then rolled flat and watered, gallons of precious water sprinkled on the lawn. Trespassing snakes must be caught and killed, monkeys chased off. The wild spirit that must be contained, shaped and, if necessary, hacked into submission.

Her father leans over her, too close, making her jump. He has a habit of sneaking up on her. His moustache tickles her neck. She can smell the rot of bad teeth.

'What are you up to?'

'Painting.'

'So I see. It's a Pitta isn't it?'

'Yes.'

'Shouldn't a young girl like you should be resting or something? Preparing for your voyage?'

'There's plenty of time for that, Daddy. Besides, I want to remember all the birds, I want to try and remember everything.'

'And this?' He picks up a book from the table, *A Guide to the Garden Birds of England,* almost knocking over her water jar and brushes.

'Yes, I thought it might help to feel at home.'

'And knowing the names of the birds will help?'

'Of course. Knowing is belonging, Daddy, you taught me that.'

'But I meant something else.'

'Yes, I know, rules and etiquette grease the wheels. But surely all knowledge is beneficial?'

'Ah,' says her father, 'rules are made to be broken, as long as you're discreet, remember that. Do as you like, just don't get caught.'

'I'll remember, but I don't think Mummy would agree.'

He perches, though he is far too big, on the arm of her chair and rests his hand on her shoulder, his fingertips caressing the skin exposed by her collar. 'Then it's our secret.'

She slides her feet from under her, shifting away from him. 'Do you want to go to England, Daddy?'

He sighs. 'We don't have much choice really, you know that. It's time to go.'

'Yes, but do you want to?'

Before he can answer, Ayah appears as if by magic, calling for her to come in. Ada jumps up, fumbles her feet into her slippers and runs towards her.

'What about your things? Her father slides his bulk into her seat.

'I'll get them later.'

Her ayah is watching her father through narrowed eyes, her hands outstretched, reaching for Ada as if pulling her to safety.

CLAIRE

It's proper exciting when the fair arrives. For the last week she's been watching as they set up the rides and stalls on Victoria banks, strung up coloured lights and bunting and covered straw bales with tarps for the seats. The banks are right at the end of her round so she lingers for a bit, letting Samson have a drink from the trough, smiling at the boys all sweaty in their vests and trousers as they winch and tighten and heft. This year she's allowed to go with Dot and Peggy, so she's fit to burst and grinning to herself like a silly mare. She's been saving the couple of bob her dad gives her each week (daylight bloody robbery, Dot says, he should give you a proper wage, but she knows they all have to jib in, pay their way and after her keep there ain't much left) so she can go on all the rides and buy sweets too.

The weather's been beautiful, all blue skies and drowsy warm, and she's run herself up a new frock from the left-over lilac cotton from Annie's bridesmaid's dresses. It's lovely it is, with cap sleeves and an almost full skirt, and she's been putting cold cream on her face and hands every evening before bed. She's a woman now, with her curse and bosoms, and she's got to take care of herself. She don't want to end up like her mother, all used up and sad, having more and more babies and none of 'em making up for George, still hardly speaking to anyone or leaving the house. Even with Annie gone and married there's no bloody room, even less now there's nine of 'em including herself. The house bursting at the seams and always the smell of damp washing and dirty nappies. No, she ain't gonna be nothing like her mother.

Mrs Riley is a new customer on her round, up the top of Maidstone Hill, near the big houses and she's a proper lady.

Very nice though, has lovely soft hands and a beautiful voice. She sounds like she's off the wireless. Always smart, even in her housecoat and slippers she has a touch of lipstick on, a little powder. Her husband's a foreman at the cement works, so she says. She's in one of the new semi-detached houses, with a front garden full of roses and pretty little pansies and the like, but she's got no airs about her, she's not stuck up. She's always got a kind word for her, last week she even complimented her on her shiny hair, Mrs Riley did laugh when she told her it was down to a final rinse in vinegar. When Claire first started delivering her weekly spuds and all that she felt common as muck next to Mrs Riley, but she's been practicing and it's not all that hard to talk nice. Not that she was dragged up, she knows her Ps and Qs, but it don't hurt to better yourself, does it? Keep yourself nice. She's decided she wants to be just like Mrs Riley, even though Dad said, 'hark at her, Miss Hoity Toity, high and mighty' when she asked for the butter putting her tongue into the Ts.

So arm in arm the three girls line up for the rides; not the octopus, that one makes her sick, but the carousel and the tea cups and the flying swings, especially the flying swings as Dot fancies the boy taking the tokens, with his wavy hair and jaunty swagger, even though all the girls know the fairground boys are off limits, beyond the pale, because you don't know where they come from or where they're going. Anyway, her skirts swish about her legs, and even though the dress is a bit tight under the arms, it does her figure a treat and she knows it. They eat toffee apples, and perch on the bales, their legs crossed at the ankles, all flouncy and perky just in case a handsome boy is watching.

As the dark draws in, all the lights switch on, glowing and swaying soft and it's like magic and they don't want to leave but it's almost time to go, so they have one last ride. They cram the three of 'em into the cradle of the Ferris wheel and clutch onto the bar holding 'em safe as they're lifted into the air, their feet kicking. At the top they watch the crowd cluster in their Sunday best in miniature, like dolls, or insects lured by the ring to be born. She tells him, 'Claire', and he smiles. He is so bloody handsome: all black hair and blue eyes that shine and crinkle and he's strong-looking too, broad shoulders and muscles, and his clothes are pressed and clean and his shoes shined. Her heart pops and jumps like a frog in a jar.

'What a pretty name for a pretty girl. I'm Dennis and this is Bill. We'll walk with you a way, will we?'

She's floating all the way home.

ADA

She has managed to give Lilian and Mummy the slip. They've made a recovery of sorts, though Lilian will no doubt succumb to her usual fits of weakness and fainting, but until the inevitable happens she has found a quiet spot on deck to take in the gentle sun and read. The ship is run rather like school, except instead of nuns, grim-faced and vicious, there are handsome sailors and uniformed members of the crew to keep them all in order. There is a strict timetable: breakfast from 7 till 9, luncheon between 12:30 and 2, dinner for which one must be appropriately dressed of course, 7 for 7:30 with dancing to follow until the band calls it a day. Finding a drink is less regimented and, should you need tea or other refreshments, you just have to ring the bell, though response times vary according to a person's position and status on ship.

The passengers are mostly English: the wives and children of the Raj, clerks, magistrates, the bureaucrats who ran the machine of Empire. They seem very large and fair to Ada, with pretty pink cheeks and loud voices. The few Anglo-Indian families, mostly from the Railway Colonies too, are all on a lower deck, though perfectly welcome at dinner, well, at least Ada has been, most of them have been too sick to attend until now. She hasn't been in the least bit lonely, away from the others, people she has known for as long as she can remember. Away from school she has become someone new, someone noticed. Someone people talk to and laugh with. She is invited to dance after dinner and she does, turning about the room with her hand demure on her partner's shoulder, smiling to herself. She is careful to behave exactly as she has been taught to, careful to watch, to learn and mimic. She is mindful that without the codes to know who and where and how, they are all lost.

'Ada! Dear!' Mrs Da Souza has spotted her, Ada sits up and marks her place in her book, suddenly finding herself surrounded by a herd of her mother's friends from the colony.

'Hello, Auntie.' She cranes her neck to see past the printed cotton frocks and wide hips for any sign of her mother. 'Are you feeling better?'

'Well, yes, for now. But it's been a trial, hasn't it?' Mrs Da Souza looks to the others for agreement. They all nod and sigh. 'Not an auspicious start, but thanks to God, we all seem to be recovering, including your beloved mother.' She crosses herself, discreetly. 'You have escaped unscathed though, glowing with health. Isn't she?' The others continue their chorus of agreement. 'Very grown up all of a sudden.'

'Thank you.' She smiles up at them, wondering what to say next and hoping a mildly uncomfortable silence might usher them along. She makes to pick up her book and excuse herself when a girl bustles past Mrs Da Souza and practically bellows, 'Hello there, you!' The girl, taller than Ada, broader too, with reddish blonde hair, holds out her hand. 'Come on, I've been looking all over for you. Excuse us, ladies.'

Ada pauses, stands up and takes the offered hand. The girl smiles goodbye at the older women and strides off, pulling Ada along, then links arms as if they were old friends. Ada looks back over her shoulder to smile at the women she's known all her life, as they shake their heads and watch her go.

'You looked like you needed rescuing. You don't know them, do you?' Before Ada can answer the girl carries on, hardly pausing for breath. 'Can you imagine? Bad enough to have been born in India, let alone be half-caste. They ought to be more careful. It's all change now: what's acceptable over there isn't at home. They'll find they aren't considered one of us anymore.' She laughs, a sound like a blunt saw dragged across piano strings.

'Yes, I suppose.' She looks back at her aunties, but they are out of sight. Shame, hot and sharp, dissolves in her throat.

'I'm Persephone by the way. I know it's awful but Mummy has a thing for Greek myths, anyway everyone calls me Percy. What about you?'

'Pardon?'

'Your name?'

'Ada.'

'Ah! That's not what I expected somehow. Well, happy to meet you, Ada.'

'Likewise.' Ada doesn't ask what this strange girl expected.

They slow down now they are out of reach of the women and stroll along the deck. Percy's sandals reveal pink nail polish; Ada's feet look gauche in comparison, but her mother would never agree to something so fast as nail polish on her girls. She tries to think of something to say, but can't, so instead she smiles at the boy polishing the brass rails. He blushes, red unfurling from the collar of his uniform to his cheeks.

Percy nudges her. 'Don't tease the poor boy, Siren!'

'I don't think I am teasing him.'

His reaction is new to her. Of course she knows other boys – Peter and Laurence Da Silva, the Harleys – but she's known them most of her life and they've certainly never looked at her like that. She shrugs her shoulders.

'Aren't you mysterious? No wonder you're the talk of the ship.'

'What do you mean?'

'At dinner, in your marvellous frock. You were the belle of the ball. I felt quite eclipsed.'

'Hardly.'

'Oh no, it's true. You looked ravishing in your golden dress, like a film star. I took one look at you and thought to myself, I have to be her friend.' Percy stops outside the piano bar. 'Let's have a gin rickey, shall we? Get acquainted. I've been so bored, I've been longing for a pal and here you are!'

48

They sit at a small table, tucked into the corner. A couple of older gentlemen look over at them, then turn away. A waiter in a black dinner suit, with a white cloth over his arm, appears at her signal. 'Two Rickeys, please.' Percy leans back in her chair and strokes the velvet covering. 'Poor old ship, all rather threadbare and past her best isn't she? Still, that's what the war did for us.' The waiter reappears and produces their drinks with a flourish. They raise their glasses and take a sip. Ada is surprised by how easy it is to drink.

'So, are you excited to go home? I haven't been back in an age, can't imagine how it is now, can you?'

'No, I suppose it's very different.' She takes another sip of her drink, ice tapping on her teeth.

'Granny said London took a pasting in the Blitz, though I hear the Savoy and Ciro's are still standing, so I'm quite happy.' She shimmies her shoulders, raising them up towards her ears, the cap sleeves of her blouse flapping like dog's ears shaking dry. Ada almost laughs but manages to swallow it with her drink. She is beginning to enjoy herself.

'Where are your people from?'

'Sorry?' She wonders how to answer this. Irish, like her grandfather? Would that cover it? That her great grandfather left Ireland aged eighteen with only his British Army uniform and a St Christopher medallion from his mother to his name? That he married a local girl? What would this strange English girl say if she tells her the truth, that she was born in Calcutta, as was her mother? What would she think if she knew her mother's mother was born in Dhaka in Bengal and her father's mother too. Would they be pals if she knew that she is a half-caste, neither this nor that, soon to understand she isn't one of them? She knows the answer. It has never been a secret, only, at home, in India, she had her place and her people were important, valuable. Daddy said they were the right hand of the British, the bridge between two cultures, though she once heard him tell her mother that they had been bred like dogs to do the work

49

the Brits didn't want to do and wouldn't trust the Indian to do either. He'd been drunk of course, the boozard.

'I mean where are you going home to?'

'Oh, Kent.' She realises the less she says, the more Percy just assumes. She's hardly lying and, besides, it's important to fit it, to belong. Isn't this what Mummy and Daddy want? Her tongue feels heavy in her mouth.

'How lovely, the Garden of England. We're back to Hampshire, and London of course. Is your father in the army? Mine's a Major General. Bloody stuffy lot. Honestly, I'm desperate to go home. I was sick of the club, sick of the wives and the sad assortment of men they paraded in front of me like skinny little colts. It's all so rowdy and uppity anyway. Daddy said that once they started killing each other it wouldn't be long before they turned on us, so best to up sticks and go home while the going is good. He's still out there of course, doing his bit. Anyway, it's all very dull.'

Ada has finished her drink. Her cheeks feel hot and her head spins. She pushes her hair from her face and leans back in her chair, feeling unexpectedly happy.

Percy watches her. 'You really are a gorgeous creature, aren't you?'

Ada laughs, delighted. She feels herself becoming exactly what Percy describes, a gorgeous English girl and, just like that, she belongs.

After a dreary lunch listening to her mother and sister list their complaints about the food, the room, the cleanliness and the reek of the ship which must be the latest cause of Lilian's headaches, Ada settles them both on sun chairs on the shaded lower deck, tucking a pillow behind her mother's head. She brings them books and orders glasses of lemonade. She wraps a shawl around her sister's shoulders; Lilian promptly pulls it off and tosses it behind her.

'What are you up to?'

'Nothing, mother. Can't I look after you?'

Lilian watches her through narrowed eyes. 'Are you in love?'

'Don't be silly, Lilian. Mummy, the steward will bring you supper on a tray in our room so you can both rest. I'll dine with the others and come straight back.'

Her mother closes her eyes, satisfied. Her sister glowers at her with a face that could turn milk sour.

She dashes back to their dark little room and squeezes into her mother's green silk gown. She can't wear her lovely damask again, what would Percy think? Her mother's dress is a little tight, but it'll have to do. Lipstick, perfume. She pins her hair up in a French pleat, but when she sees her reflection in the mirror she changes her mind and brushes it out again. She feels strange: excited and frightened and sad all at once. But it won't do to sit and wallow, and besides, the longer she dallies the more likely it is that her mother and sister will return and catch her out.

'Here she is, I promised you she would come! Ada darling, rescue us!' Percy, dressed in a curious velvet gown that seems to blend in with the upholstery of her seat, is surrounded by a small group of men. One of them leaps to his feet and offers her his chair. They are all almost identical in their dinner suits with their pale, bland faces. She smiles and nods and lets each one press her hand as Percy introduces them, a collection of Georges and Edwards and a Charles. One of them pours her a glass of champagne from the bottle chilling in a silver bucket on the table. She sips, the cool liquid prickling her tongue.

'Darling, we were so bored without you. Won't you play something for us?' Percy beams at the men, her large teeth glinting in the low light. 'Wouldn't that be marvellous, Edward?' They all nod and murmur agreement and turn to look at her expectantly like a hungry crowd of macaques. She hesitates, not knowing the form for a situation like this. Would she be making a spectacle of herself? Showing off, unladylike. She decides and finishes her drink in one swallow. She stands, to which Percy claps her hands excitedly, the Edward next to her pulling back her seat. At the piano she runs her fingers over the keys, a loose arpeggio, testing the notes. She sits, thinks for a moment, then starts to play.

TAMARA

'Your roots are showing.'

'Pardon?' She touches her hair. It isn't dyed. Then she understands as Christopher and the couple opposite laugh.

'It's pronounced *suPERlative* not *super-LAtive*.' Christopher uses sipping his wine as a punctuation point.

'Right,' she says. As if it isn't enough to know what the word means and how to use it in a sentence. Lately he likes to out her, calls her Mrs Malaprop, or replies to her texts by correcting her grammar. Maybe not that often, maybe only occasionally. She colludes in belittling herself to save face. These are his friends, this tall, casually gorgeous couple. Henry works with Christopher at the agency and they insist on calling each other Hank and Topher like they're rich East Coast Americans in a John Cheever story, and Margot, Henry's girlfriend, is in arts admin. It's clear to Tamara that they already think she's a loser so she has nothing to lose.

'You know the first time I ever met my grandmother the first thing she did was correct how I said hyperbole. I said hyperbowl. What an idiot!' She laughs and lays her hand on Christopher's; his eyes widen in circles of horror.

In the pause she is suddenly very aware of the dink and scrape of cutlery on plates and the hum of voices, the waiters moving between the tables. The light splitting on glassware and diverting in sharp angles across the restaurant. She has never been here before, but she's read about it in the Food section of the Sunday paper. She looks down at her plate, and for a second is surprised to see she is eating some sort of pasta. She doesn't remember ordering it.

'Wait, rewind, what?' Margot leans on the table, closer to her. 'When you *met* your grandma? How do you *meet* your grandma? Didn't you always know her?'

'Not that one, I didn't meet her till I was fourteen.'

'Seriously?' Henry, Hank, chips in. He is leaning forward too, they're interested.

'Yeah. I didn't know that side of the family when I was growing up.'

'Wow. Can I ask why?'

Christopher has slumped in his seat and is looking bored, as if he might have to reach for his phone.

'My parents were just teenagers when I was born.'

'How young?'

'Sixteen or so.'

'Jesus, that's young.'

'Was it hard?'

'I didn't know any different I suppose. I thought my dad was in the—'

'She grew up on a council estate too, you know.' Christopher leans forward. 'It's an inspiring tale of a self-made cockney sparrow done good. Isn't it, darling?' He puts his arm around her and squeezes. 'She's almost got rid of the chip on her shoulder.'

'Wow,' repeats Margot, 'you can't tell. Can you, Henry?'

'You can when she visits her hometown, or when she's drunk or angry. You should hear how her accent changes depending on who she's talking to. It's hilarious, like she's Eliza Doolittle.'

Her mother tells her, '*Ain't* ain't a word.' She should say *isn't* instead. She reminds her: 'it's not bu'ah, it's butter. Say your T's.' Even though her mother doesn't press her tongue to every letter she says, even though the other kids will call her a snob or posh or something much worse. Her mother says, 'You're better than all this. I want you to have everything I never did. We'll show 'em who's common, won't we babe? Sod 'em. You will be a lady. You'll be special.'

Maybe it's the last argument they have. It should've been, or will be as it's the one we remember. They leave, walk home, his arm draped around her shoulder. 'That was a good night but you didn't need to do that, you know.'

'What?'

'Embarrass us all with your self-pitying little anecdotes.'

'Who did I embarrass?'

'Me, you embarrassed me. You were wallowing in self-pity.'

'I wasn't wallowing; I was trying to laugh at myself.'

'Well, you dominated the conversation. No one could get a word in.'

'They were asking questions.'

'Which you answered.'

'What should I have done?'

'Redirected them, turned the conversation around. And you were weird.'

'What do you mean?'

'Just be yourself. Stop trying so hard.'

'I'm not.'

'Be the you I know.'

'But I am. I was.'

'You're impossible, do you know that?'

'I'm sorry, I'm not trying to be.'

'You know it's really hard to get to know you, you're so closed down, all surface and pretence. When you don't know someone you can't love them. It's impossible.'

'What do you mean? You don't love me?'

'And the irony is you're in communications... Some communicator.'

'I'm sorry.'

'Stop saying that.'

'Then what shall I say? That you embarrassed me? That you're fucking spiteful and cruel? Is that better? Is that what you want? Is that enough communication?'

'You're drunk, and hysterical.'

'Actually I'm not drunk, but I should be, living with you.'

'There's nothing worse than a drunk woman.'

'You've had way more than me but that's ok, right? Because you're a man, and you can take it and a woman who drinks is unladylike and excessive, isn't she?'

To prove his point, she vomits. Doubled over, folded up small. Her body betraying her. She leaves a pool of slick bubbles sparkly in the gutter.

CLAIRE

Up before everyone else, she's swept out the range and got the bleeder lit, the water on to boil for Dad and Bert, who's taken Annie's place in the shop now she's in the family way and not having to work. Out in the yard Samson's tacked up and ready, teeth grinding at the bit, his iron shoes clattering and clashing on the cement like one of them tap dancers. The cart's stocked and the hens fed; she'll be off and out before her mother and the little uns have roused, but not before a nice bit of bread and dripping and a good mug of tea and perhaps a spot of bacon to see her right. She's keeping her chin up, all things considered.

It's almost spring again and, aside from going to the pictures with Dot of a Saturday, it's been a long and miserable winter. They had to pile coats on top of their blankets, and there was even ice on the inside of the windows in January. It's not so much the cold that she hates, but the long dark and the damp that gets right into your bones and screws you up into a hunch, like a beetle scuttling along. She never thought she'd see that Den or his pal again, she's not the type of girl boys come courting, not with her skinny flanks and lumpy nose, not her. Who'd want her? But she was wrong, weren't she? A week after the fair, he came knocking for her and asking for permission to take her out, shaking her dad's hand. And just to clinch it he only brought a couple ounces of pear drops for her mum and the kids, didn't he! Then it was shy walks, and fish and chips, and bags of sherbet dip and rhubarb and custards and the Saturday matinee and a bus trip to the Strand for ice cream and a deck chair overlooking the estuary, which wasn't the same as the seaside but beggars can't be choosers, and he even met her at the end of her round and helped with brushing Samson and putting the cart away. She can't believe her luck, girl like her and a fella like him and then he's gone, signed up and handsome in his RAF blue serge posted somewhere up north and why would she be surprised that she was alone again?

So yeah, it had been a long and miserable winter, missing him, but he'd kept his word and sent her letters, hadn't he? How he was learning and getting a trade and would be able to take care of her when he got out. He told her about his three meals a day, and how his boots and uniform were new to him, and only his, and how he had plenty of fags and beer, and how clean it all was and the marvels of an engine and the lift of a plane and how even the officers were all right. And he wrote about love. A love of her own. So no matter how much her mum and dad run her down, no matter that she'll never be good enough and that they run her ragged with the cleaning and the washing and the working and the doing, she's loved and she just thinks about how he looked at her, how he held her close and the pure weight of him against her and she knows everything will be all right.

TAMARA

With only ten miles to go until the junction we need, she stops at the services. Parks the car in the short stay car park and enters the restaurant building. An escalator takes her up to a travellator that sweeps her and a line of other passengers along the five-hundred-metre corridor to the concession stands. She tries to walk but can't get past the other people who block her way like clots in an artery. Some kind of music is administered by speakers embedded in the ceiling. She turns to look out of the window, but the smoked glass discloses only the impression of the rushing cars below them. She must be passive: stock still, not looking, not thinking. At the food court she takes a minute to choose which stand to buy something from. She chooses, though the choice is pointless because it's all the same, and takes her sandwich and coffee over to a table. She chews the cold, tasteless sandwich, leaving half in the plastic shell. She could be anywhere. The plastic-topped tables, the harsh lighting, the plastic plants, the pine-scented disinfectant, the tiled floor and the signage are the same everywhere.

Everyone wearing the same clothes, the same tired expressions, eating the same mass-produced over-processed food. Children on their tablets, zip zap bing. Music crystallised like sugar. There's never any peace, never any quiet. Stimulation is constant. Everywhere could be anywhere. She sits with the other people, men and women, children, the elderly. In family groups and couples and alone. A crowd of women sit together and sip coffee. On a coach tour maybe. She makes sure to steer clear of their sharp, happy edges, sits alone, eyes down.

In a darkened recess there are a few slot machines, and a driving game for people who can't stop navigating and speeding across the void. Human expressions at their most intense morph and imitate each other. Laughter caught mid-shriek is a scream of pain. Joyous celebration mimics violent rioting. Humans are always on the verge, that spasm of violence just under the surface. Mutable. Barely contained.

A woman cleans the floor, her black hair in a bun at the nape of her neck. She wears a green overall and rubber clogs. White socks. We watch as she moves from one side of the eating area to the other and then back again. The filth ever-recurring. A domestic Sisyphus. We know what that's like. We remember. Her mother was a cleaner. Then a home help. 'It never ends,' her mother used to say, 'a woman's work is never done. I clean other people's filth and shit and then come home to yours.'

She gets up to leave, making sure to brush her crumbs into her cup and throwing it all away in the bin. We taught her well, no one cleans up after her; she knows her place, she doesn't have ideas above her station. As she exits she passes a group of men – T-shirts, jeans, a wedding ring or two, paunches and receding hair, fogged by sour booze, old enough to know better – and is told to smile, love, it might never happen. She ignores them, and is rewarded with a 'miserable bitch', and just in case she had any illusions, 'ugly cunt' tops it off. Some things don't change.

It's been a while since anyone even talked about her mother, since she heard the words 'your mum' in a conversation. She does her best to never mention her, she does her best to forget her.

'Are you sure?' she asks the woman.

'Yes,' she says – her voice soft, warm. She imagines her to be mumsy, attractive, plump and loved. She's most likely wrong, as she so often is. 'Yes, you are listed as her next of kin. It's you she wants.'

Time re-pleats itself, concertinas, folding over the absences so they tuck unseen behind a seamless presence. She has always been her mother's daughter, after all. It's not a lie, just a simple revision. It's possible her mother does want her. It's possible she has imagined the years apart. She sits down, suddenly sick, her head throbbing. This is a new sensation. Until recently she was never ill, never sick, never made a fuss. She got on with it, had to, it was required of her.

Numb, slow to respond. Pain, emotional or physical, occurs to her hours, sometimes days after the upset. She moves through the world with an added layer of material insulating her from sensation. Most people think she is inauthentic, putting on a front, a brave face. Unreachable, phony. The truth is, she second guesses every moment. Questions her every gesture, word and feeling. She polices herself, holds herself to a standard imposed before she was even conscious. A way of staying safe, likeable. Keeping herself daughtered to her mother, who might turn her back and run away at any moment. And now, it's a habit, a reflex. She must maintain the likeable front. Because behind it all she is unlovable, filthy, shameful.

The room shifts underneath her, its angles recompose, pulling the light in new directions. A current flares under her skin. She feels. Something unknown. Uncertain, she calls Pav, who picks up, sounding surprised.

'Hey.'

'You busy?'

'It's ok, what's up?'

'I've just had the weirdest call.'

'Are you ok? You sound strange.'

'Erm, I don't know. I just... fuck.'

'What's happened?'

'I just had a call from a hospital. About my mum.'

'Your mum? I thought she was...it doesn't matter. What did they say?'

'She's dying. The woman said she asked for me.'

'Oh God, that's terrible. Do you want me to come with you?'

'I'm not going there.'

'Why?'

'Because what's the point?'

'Because she's your mum, and she's dying. How can you not go?'

'Because we hate each other. Because I don't care about her.'

Pav sighs. 'People say stupid shit when they're angry. This is your chance to fix it. To move on.'

'Yeah. Maybe.'

'She asked for you. That's means something.'

'Maybe she didn't, she just put me down as her next of kin.'

'What's the difference? It's her way of reaching out to you.'

'Or to tell me she wishes I'd never been born for one last time.'

She thinks about the forms HR has her check and amend every year.

She leaves the emergency contact blank. She used to joke it was the only reason to stay married. To have someone there, a constant answer to someone's question.

'I think you should go.'

'Maybe. Oh God, I don't know what to do. I haven't seen her for ages and still she manages to fuck me up.'

'Listen I have to go to a meeting, but I can get out after and come with, if you want.'

'No, it's all right, don't worry. I'll sort something out.'

'Call me, ok?'

'Yeah, thanks.'

She doesn't move for a long time. Her ears continue to ring.

On a night bus home, where has she been? Out. Drinks somewhere, dinner perhaps, the cinema maybe. She chooses a seat near the driver. Tries to sit with authority, back straight, alert, so the drunks and the nut jobs don't bother her. She thinks she sees her mother, in the seat ahead. Is sure it's her. The same slant of shoulders, the straight hair and in profile, when the woman turns to look out of the rain-pocked window, the same small chin and long nose. She shudders as if she's seen a ghost, but her mother is not dead. Wasn't dead. Will be dead.

ADA

It doesn't matter how many times their mother insists, Lilian shouts, she won't get used to England. How can she? Why would she want to get used to rows and rows of ugly little houses with their chimney pots all lined up, all grey, grey, grey? The way the English stop and stare at them as they go about their business. Though she hates to admit it, for once Ada agrees with her sister and, despite trying her best, so does their poor mother. Grey sky, grey paving stones, grey buildings. Even the people look grey, their faces pale and drawn, red flaky skin around their noses, chapped lips and thin hair. Everyone and everything looks the same, as if they are just reproduced from a weary old pattern.

This will never be home. They've left everything and everyone they know behind. Though Ada wonders now how much of what she thought was theirs actually belonged to someone else. It turns out their furniture was rented, even her piano, which is just as well as none of it would fit in the tiny house Daddy has found them here. It's stuck in the middle of a long row, with no wall to separate it from the street and only a tiny garden at the back of the house. It has two rooms downstairs, a sitting room with feeble gas fire and a damp patch on the ceiling the colour of turmeric, a dining room with wallpaper peeling from the wall and a kitchen which, oddly, is inside the house. There are two bedrooms upstairs, a tiny box room for Grandfather and a bathroom which apparently is a luxury even though the enamel bath is chipped and stained. Nail heads bulge from the floorboards and rip her stockings. There is nowhere for servants to sleep. There will be no servants, poor Mummy. Her father says she is not the Memsahib anymore and must learn to cook and clean for herself. That they should think themselves lucky they could get the papers to come here; from the looks the neighbours give them, not everyone agrees with him that luck was on their side.

And it's cold. So damp and cold with endless rain; the only thing interesting is how many different ways there are for it to rain, unlike home and the drenching monsoon, so abundant and glorious and life affirming. In England there is drizzle; a lacklustre, mean rain that penetrates the bones with its cold but doesn't soak; mizzle where the rain drops are so small they confuse gravity and are almost a fine mist; there's the needling, sharp, icy rain that is usually accompanied by a hectoring wind and there's the type that has large weighty drops that saturate and make the unpaved areas of ground a thick sludge of mud. There are months of rain it seems. Months of water. So much of it that none of it is precious.

It is hard to believe that this grey, shrinking place is the home of Shakespeare, Chaucer, Queen Victoria and Wordsworth; she can't imagine being inspired to anything much here. Grandpa insists that the countryside is lovely, but Lilian is adamant that's claptrap, they all saw the countryside from the train after they docked at Southampton and it was all dreary and portioned into little squares of churned up soil. Everything in this country is cramped and ugly. And the food is disgusting. At least Ada managed to avoid Percy and her set when they docked, God knows she couldn't have borne the shame if she'd had to introduce them all to her mother and sister; and even though it's bad luck to lose her only friend in this country it's better to save face and make the best of it.

It's also her rotten luck to have to share her bedroom with Lilian, who refuses to leave her bed or even open the thin curtains. On the other hand her father pays her less attention, in fact keeps his distance. Ada is sitting at the little desk that doubles as their dressing table working on an exercise in her Pitman's text book. Lilian is in bed, the heavy woollen blankets pulled up to her chin. The blankets are itchy and have given her a rash on her face and neck but she refuses to pull them down. Lilian has a perfectly good chin, a very nice shaped chin, but one would never know it because she pulls it into her neck in disapproval of the world. As if she is pulling her face as far away from what offends her as she can. This action has the side effect of giving the illusion of protruding top teeth. If only she liked the world and herself in it, she'd have a nice smile. A shriek billows up like a cloud of laundry steam from the kitchen below. Ada puts down her pencil.

'Oh dear, that sounds ominous.'

'Poor Mummy, she can't even make toast.'

'It's really not that hard. I don't know why she makes such a song and dance about it.'

'It sounds like she's crying down there.'

'She's always crying.'

'That's because it's always raining, she's all watery in sympathy.'

'Perhaps we should go and help.'

'Perhaps we should, but we might just get in the way and make things worse.'

'I don't think things can get any worse. If she makes rumble tumble again Daddy will be furious.'

'Yuk. It's not even made with real eggs and the war's been over for ages.'

'For pity's sake, Lilian, it's only three years yet.'

'That's long enough surely. I think it's because they're so lazy that food is still rationed and they haven't mended the bomb damage. Lazy and greedy. Even their hens are lazy.'

'I think it's more complicated than that, Lilian.'

'Really? Why then?'

'Supply lines or something. I don't know.'

'Well, the English are lazy and greedy, that man today proved it. Wait till Daddy finds out she has to register at a new grocer's because of that ghastly shopkeeper.'

'She was rude! She spoke to him like he was a punkah wallah.'

'He pretended he couldn't understand what she was saying, so she had to shout. Nasty little man, thinking he's superior; of course he knows what custard apples are. Anyway, who does he think he is, calling us names and saying he won't serve coloureds?'

'Everyone thinks they're superior: the whites think they're better than the Indians, the Indians think they're better than the whites, the English think they're the cream of the crop and mother believes she is better than them all. It's all nonsense.'

A handful of grit tumbles down their chimney into the little grate and onto the rug.

'It's not nonsense. It's miserable here and dirty, they live like pigs. I hate it. We weren't coloured at home, and we weren't poor either.'

'We're not at home are we? We just have to make the best of it.'

'Easy for you to say. Look at you, Miss English Rose.'

'I'm not arguing with you, Lil. Are you coming to help or not?'

'Not. I'm too cold.'

'Fine, I'll go.' Ada walks along the narrow passage towards the stairs, trying to imagine she is on the verandah at home but it's no use, the jasmine flowers just evaporate in the damp gloom.

CLAIRE

Side by side with Den, her shoes pinching her something rotten. She's had to borrow Annie's smart coat and, though she don't quite fill it, she looks half decent just so long as she can keep it on, as her dress has seen better days.

He sneaks a little squeeze of her hand as the coffin is lowered into the ground. Side by side with Den like she's his missus, one of the family. The spread fingers of horse chestnut leaves pat at the air above them, a dunnock warbles and whistles, little crowds of cheery daffodils nod in the grass. No one, not even Den's mother standing alone by the grave, seems all that upset, he was a mean old git by all accounts, and as Den said, he was only his stepdad, so there's no love lost, but still you'd think one of them could push out a tear or two, for the sake of decency if nothing else.

Back at the house, which is nice and clean and has a good carpet and a matching settee and arm chair but she doesn't want to seem rude so can't look around too much, he introduces her to his mother, his arm around her shoulder. 'This is my Claire.'

'So I see,' his mother looks her up and down like she's something the cat dragged in. 'How long are you on leave for?'

'Have to be back in barracks by tomorrow, mother.'

'Well, you'll not be stopping here, I've no room.' With that she gives Claire a last look over and stumps out, leaving Claire's practiced condolences hanging in the air like cankered apples. She swallows hard and just like that she feels as ugly as sin inside and out.

'Don't mind her,' says a girl who can only be his sister, all shiny dark hair and blue eyes as she gives Den a cuddle. 'Her bark is worse than her bite. I'm Shirley, by the way, his favourite little sister, and I know who you are, he never stops talking about you.'

'My favourite pain in the backside more like. Make yourself useful and go and get us a cuppa.'

The cup rattles on the saucer, but she sits nice, knees together, her coat unbuttoned but still on, even though it seems everyone keeps telling her she won't feel the benefit when she's outside. She speaks when spoken to, smiles when she should, but even so she knows what they're all thinking, she's not stupid, she can see behind all the polite chatter and questions. She's not good enough for him, they're all wondering what he sees in her, being common as muck and an eyetie too and the knowing hurts, it doesn't matter what he says, the knowing stays like a nasty worm eating at her insides. She feels sick with the knowing that one day he'll see her for what she is and it's a sickness and love and a frenzy that will carry her away, and just like that she's made her bed and will have to lie in it.

Stripped down to her bra and petticoat Claire is washing in front of the fire. Her mother is silent in her chair, her fingers twisting and pulling at each other in her lap as Claire soaps up the flannel and scrubs her face, neck and behind her ears. Dad is out as usual, seeing his fancy woman, Daphne Norton, if you listen to what the old cows say gathered outside the bakers, their lips pressed tight to stop them contaminating themselves from the filth they spread.

Bert's at his evening class, learning his book-keeping. There's so many blokes about now he's got to be competitive, he says, if he's going to better himself. All them heroes looking for their old jobs back, better jobs, wounded or not. Dad says they ain't heroes, that doing your duty is the least you can do, and if they're bloody heroes what's he? Keeping a roof over all their heads and feeding them and clothing them. No one gives him a medal. They know better than to say anything to him, miserable sod. Bert thinks he's just annoyed he missed out on both wars and his chance to prove himself.

She's just put the kiddies to bed, though June is almost fourteen and getting lippy so she hardly counts and should be shifting for herself by rights. There's the four youngest girls top and tail in the old double bed, two in the bunk bed under her, plus the three boys in the box room. Won't be long now before she's married and can get out. Another year or so, give or take, Den says, not long till he's finished his service and with a trade too. She's buying bits and pieces for her bottom drawer, tea towels, bed linen and the like, and he's putting a bit aside each week in the post office. It's beginning to feel like it might happen, though she tries not to get her hopes up, just in case. For all she knows he's got a girl on the side where he is, but what she don't know can't hurt her and when she asked him in a letter if he had another sweetheart he wrote back and told her not to be so daft. She does her best to rein in her worst imaginings.

Undoing her bra she soaps under her arms, across her chest and under her bosom. Her mother, still in her chair, gasps. She turns, dropping the cloth in the water. 'What's up, Mamma?' Her mother is staring at her body. Instinctively she wraps her arms around herself, holding herself close. Her mother gets up, heaving herself out of the chair and steps towards her. She don't move, won't move. Let her come closer, she's not scared of her. Her mother reaches for her wrists and pulls her arms down by her side. Her mother is much stronger than she looks. Her mother stares at her then pinches one of her breasts, hard.

'You stupid girl. You stupid shameless girl. How far along are you?'

It dawns on her that it's true then, it's real, because a bit of her hoped that if she ignored it, it would just go away, even though deep down she knows it's wishful thinking.

ADA

Finally, summer has emerged, rising like an island from the watery depths of winter. Ada is sitting in the park, soft grass tickling the backs of her legs. She has kicked off her shoes, her toes tipped with a forbidden bright pink. She has finished her lunch of corned beef sandwiches and is sketching a Cinnabar moth to send to Ayah. She only has coloured pencils, but still it looks quite striking; the hot red contrasts with the black, more like a creature from home than one would imagine here in England. She is beginning to like it here. The summer improves things with its gentle warmth and bright air. She feels as if she is unravelling, standing straight after a long winter spent in a mean hunch against the cold. At least she can get out of the house and away from the family. She is nearly finished with secretarial school, too; she just has a couple of exams left and she can find a job. She won't be sorry to say goodbye to the catty girls with their voices that sound as if they are being squeezed through their noses. They call her Lady Muck, and comment on her accent and her manners, her clothes and hair. They even take exception to her typing speed, as if it's her doing that they are so slow and clumsy. It's all quite amusing, because they imagine that the opinion of dumpy, poorly educated, fat-ankled girls would matter to her. Which it doesn't. They're all obsessed with Princess Elizabeth, her husband and their new baby. Some of them still talk about listening to the wedding on a wireless set and how magical it all seemed. Which perhaps it was, but she doesn't know because she didn't listen to it. It doesn't matter, she's seen the photographs in magazines and it looked pretty ordinary to her; but the way these girls talk it's as if they might be future princesses, marrying a duke, giving birth to a prince; they discuss details about clothing and behaviour and the naming of children as if they were close friends of the royal family, or at least intimately connected, not soon-to-be-typists in a small town.

She listens to the birds, whose song is a timid melody rather than the more raucous demands of the birds at home. She wonders what secrets they keep. Everything is smaller, milder here. One must pay closer attention to see its charms. She watches as a pair of wrens flit and call to their babies who clumsily emerge, one by one, from a crevice in the old stone wall that surrounds the small park. Bees crawl into foxglove flowers, then bump and tumble off to another crop. A magpie eyes the discarded crusts of her sandwich, stalking at the edge of a boundary it has decided on, keeping guard until she goes and it is safe to grab her leavings. She tries to smudge her blue and black pencil markings together to create the lustre of its dark feathers but it's impossible. She throws the crusts to it, and it snatches them up and takes off.

She finishes her letter to Ayah, which is mostly sketches so that Ayah can enjoy those at least until her son, Dinesh, is home to read it to her. It takes ages for the letters to get there, and even longer to get a reply, written by Dinesh of course. Her mother says Ayah has a new job, a new life, and is too busy for her letters, but Ada is certain that if she could only learn to write in Hindi then it wouldn't be so difficult. Ayah can't read English, but how and where will Ada find a class in England? It strikes her that this is absurd but, like all these thoughts that prickle and demand more than she cares to give, she pushes it away. Ayah's letters mention very little of home, only that Ayah is in good health and that she misses them all; that so and so has left the village or that a neighbour has been blessed with a baby. Ada knows better than to ask about the troubles or how the families who stayed behind have fared and she knows better than to tell Ayah how much she longs to come home.

In Ayah's last letter there was a pressed hibiscus, its petals dried a dark red around the yellow stamen and seeds with a short note reminding her to be good and careful and brave. It is a message that conveys more than simple words and one she understands. Ayah took her once – and only once because father found out and put a stop to it – to make Puja to Kali. It hadn't been too far, just across the bridge over the Hooghly River with its huge fish, but as she was only a child it seemed miles from home.

The temple buildings with their curved roofs were reached by climbing up steep stone steps; there was a large bathing tank to the right. It was busy, and she followed Ayah through the crowd into the main temple, bowing as she bowed and kneeling by her side. Ayah closed her eyes and began to chant, the words almost sung under her breath. Ada watched her lips forming the words, the tip of her tongue, her eyelashes resting on her cheek; she rested her hand on Ayah's lap, needing to be felt by Ayah, even if she wasn't seen. There were many other women in the temple, some sitting in silence, some murmuring too. Men were not allowed. Incense smoke spiralled in dry coils from sticks pressed between the palms of their hands and placed at the foot of the Goddess by the priestesses. Ayah bent and pressed her forehead to the floor then sat up and patted Ada on her knee.

'Stay here.'

Ada nodded and watched, her heart beating hard as Ayah approached ferocious Kali with her three eyes, long gold tongue and four gold hands – one was holding a scimitar, one clutched the severed head of a man by his hair, while the other two gave blessings to her followers. Ayah bowed to the Goddess again, then from her basket she offered little dishes of rice and salt and a bunch of red hibiscus flowers tied with a red cotton ribbon. Ada held her breath: the sword the goddess clutched was just inches from Ayah's head. The goddess didn't strike but kept watch over them, her right foot pressing Shiva into the ground. She had seen Kali before, but only on the small altar in Ayah's room, never like this, where she was huge and looked alive and hungry. Outside the temple Ayah asked her if she was afraid.

'No, Ayah. Well, only a little.'

'Don't be afraid, Ada-Priya. Kali is our mother; she was born to save heaven and earth from evil demons.'

'But she has killed a man.'

'Not a man, she killed many demons and sometimes it is necessary to kill in order to save others. Things have to end, so that something new and beautiful can be born, that is what Kali tells us.'

'What about the man she is standing on? Is he dead?'

'No, that is Shiva, her husband, he is just receiving her blessing and calming her rage.'

'But Ayah, ladies don't fight and kill. They aren't strong enough.'

'That is what the men would like us to believe. Kali Ma reminds us of our strength. Now let's eat a little before we go home.'

'Ayah?'

'Yes, Missy Baba?'

'Will Kali Ma be my mother too?'

Ayah stroked the child's hair back from her face, pinching her nose. 'If you are a good girl.'

'I try.'

'I know. Now, let's eat and rest.'

They sat in the shade to rest before the walk home, her head in Ayah's lap and she drifted off to sleep listening to the women talking and laughing. The sun turned the river a supple bronze.

She keeps the pressed hibiscus in her diary. She wishes it were easier to be brave and accept change, though she refuses to whimper about it and has decided she isn't in the least bit lonely or in need of friends. She realises that she can feel what she tells herself to feel; except for the sly feeling that something in England has contaminated her, not a disease as such, but a confusion of substance. She has taken to writing her diary in shorthand, though she has modified the rather simple Pitman's she has been taught and created her own version as a precaution against Lilian's prying when she eventually finishes the same course. The new marks help her describe this new reality, a reality she has decided upon. It is not a new language, only a mangled form of her old one. One that no longer fits this place or who she might become. What she writes is what she must be, what she will be.

TAMARA

The girl is eleven, her hair in long plaits. She wants her hair cut, like her friends. She hates having it brushed, hates having it washed, the shampoo stinging her eyes. It hurts. She looks like a baby with her ribbons and ponytails and spam-head forehead the boys at school like to slap. She waits until her mother comes to tuck her into bed and, just as she is kissing her cheek good night, plucks up the courage to ask, 'Please can I have my hair cut in a bob like Tracey?'

Sitting rigid, the mother's hands tighten over the sheets. She is as still as a statue; the child holds her breath. Waiting. Her mother's eyes slowly fill with tears. She blinks and the tears roll like stones over her face and onto her sweatshirt.

'See how you've upset me? You know just how to hurt me, don't you? What's wrong with your beautiful hair? You are so ungrateful.' She tugs one of the girl's braids. 'This is the prettiest thing about you.' Her mother slams the door behind her.

When she gets up in the morning she leaves her two long plaits behind on the pillow. She screams. Her mother opens the bedroom door.

'Isn't that what you wanted? I thought you'd be pleased.'

She doesn't cry as she tries to push the hacked edges of her hair behind her ears. She is learning fast that she ought not to ask for what she wants.

At first he throws things, a drinking glass, a picture frame, her laptop – at the wall. He smashes a window with his fist. He punches the wall just by her head. Then he begs, insults, rages, cajoles (no one else will want you) and sulks.

'I've never hit you,' he says. 'You can't say I'm violent.'

76

He screams in her face, spraying spit everywhere, 'You know you're fucking insane, you're mental.'

A strange and yet conventional piece of theatre. We've seen it all before. No one will believe she's doing it, her, leaving him. But she will, she does. Only her mother isn't surprised – Tamara's a quitter, has no stamina. Hasn't got what it takes to make a marriage work.

It's easier than she imagines. When it hurts so much the next stage is numbness, a paralysis of the nerves, an overwhelming of the senses that leads to a shutdown, like the overheating of a nuclear reactor. Dead and buried. Half of their friends unfollow her, some even go so far as to block her on Facebook. It's fine, she thinks, he's entitled to claim his digital social life. Divorcing is simple. She leaves, takes nothing. Leaves him with his X Box, his guitar and the set of Le Creuset pans he loved so much. Starts again. Easy. It wasn't easy. Isn't easy. But she has Pav, her friend. We might have confused some of the details with other stories, but no matter, they're all the same in the long run.

CLAIRE

Bert stops their dad beating the baby out of her. She ain't noticed how big he's got, big enough to hold the old man back, suddenly a man himself. He couldn't stop their dad spitting on her though, down there on the floor curled up to protect her stomach, or calling her and her baby names. Annie won't speak to her with her fancy husband, nor her mother of course, but that don't stop 'em expecting her to do their bidding though. She's soiled, dirty, but good enough to boil their filthy washing up on the copper and run it through the mangle, good enough to mind the kids and scrub the floors. Her dad keeps her out on the round too, probably hoping the walking and carrying will rid her of it. That'll be why they've not sent her away to the Catholic Home for Fallen Girls, she's too useful at home.

News about her being in the family way has spread like lice, but most people are kind, or at least don't say nothing to her face about it, and she has a young man who will come and marry her and ain't lots of girls got caught out like this and were carrying their first when they tied the knot. Only Miss Thomas in the haberdashers refused to serve her and all she wanted was some buttons, but Dot, God love her, went storming in there and give the old biddy what for. They did laugh about it, the two of 'em, thick as thieves. Still, it rankles a bit.

She's bone tired, the heaviness deep inside her more than the baby, more than the backache and the headaches and the thickening of her legs and body and face. At first she's sure Den will come, that it will all be all right, he loves her, don't he? But there's been no more letters, not even a postcard. She tells herself he's busy, that he's working hard to come and take her with him, but weeks have passed and she's given up looking out for him and his letters and crying herself to sleep. He's just like all the rest, more fool her for believing different. Her belly hardens and she is harder, too, pulling herself up straight as she can, belly thrust out, none of that round-shouldered, eyes-downcast penitence for her. She's as brazen as her dad says she is. It's just her and the baby and no matter what they say she's eighteen and they can't make her give the baby up. She'll find a way. She imagines all the love her baby will bring her and knows she will find a way; she won't go cap in hand to anyone.

She's as a big as a house, ready to drop, but still she's doing the round, plodding alongside Samson who looks about ready to drop himself. Poor old fella, she coos to him, they'll be sending us both off to the knacker's yard soon. Just as well she's still out there though, because that's where Shirley finds her, weighing up poor old Lucy Ridley's sprouts and peas.

'Thank God,' she says, 'I've been out here looking for you for days.'

'Well, here I am,' she says, 'you've found me.' Her belly between them, the baby tugging and turning under her ribs.

'Can I touch it?'

'If you want.'

Gingerly, Shirley reaches her hand towards her.

'It don't bite,' she says and taking the soft manicured hand presses it against her. The baby kicks out, making Shirley jump.

TAMARA

She is starting a new school, with a new name. This time they aren't hiding from an old dad but are making a fresh start with a new one. He wants her to wear his name like a bell around her neck. The other children have already made friends and stand two by two, holding hands. She stands at the back of the line. Waiting to go into class. The other kids say she smells and whisper nasty things. One of them says, 'I bet she gets free school dinners,' loud enough for everyone to hear. They all laugh.

CLAIRE

Bert tries to calm her down, trying to put his arm around her shoulders and keep her steady.

'Leave off, Bert,' she says, 'or I'll swing for you too, God help me I will.'

He steps back.

'It's lies,' her father says, shrugging. 'All lies.'

'Is it really? Shall I call her in then? Cos she's out there and she told me a pretty tale, let me tell you.' She points to Shirley, standing outside the shop, holding on to Samson where she'd left them. 'I've heard it all, Dad, and you disgust me. You really do. Now I want my money and my letters and I want them right now or I'll call the police. D'you hear me? I'll have you, you bastard.'

'Call the police,' he says. 'You can't prove nothing. Anyway, if I took anything it's because it's mine. Owed to me after all the trouble you've caused, you trollop.'

So she lamps him one so hard she knocks him sideways. The small crowd that's gathered outside to watch start their clucking and wittering, their cherrying and mucking.

'Had a good look, have ya?' she shouts before Bert drags her out.

ADA

Mr. Robson, unlike the other men in the office, is always so beautifully dressed his suits and shirts must be handmade. His hair is oiled back and his moustache perfectly straight above his rather girlish top lip. Also unlike the other men in the office, he is always perfectly respectful to her, never once making a sly comment about her legs, or staring at her bosom or pressing up against her in the corridor. He is a gentleman or as close to it as she might encounter in a paper mill, with the exception of poor Mr. Miller, but he hardly counts.

'How do you like it?'

'It's rather good, thank you.' She finishes the soup and places her spoon carefully at an angle in the bowl, then smooths the napkin over her knees. 'Thank you for inviting me to lunch.' It is only a small, rather shabby restaurant, with mostly businessmen lunching and smoking around them. The tablecloth is thin paper, disintegrating in damp circles under their glasses of water and wine, and the dark red curtains droop despondently from the rails over the windows. The waiter takes their empty bowls, clattering the spoons as he turns.

'I'm glad you could come. As I said in the office, I want to discuss your future with us.'

'Indeed. Thank you.' She takes a sip of her wine to curtail the urge to say thank you yet again; it tastes of vinegar but, as she is by no means a connoisseur, she's not sure if it's supposed to. She takes another sip and it tastes a little better. This is her first visit to a restaurant since they came to England and she feels just a little giddy. The waiter returns and slides their plates of lamb chops and mashed potato in front of them. A small mound of pale peas threatens to topple into her gravy.

'Anything else?' The waiter tucks his hands behind his back as if he is hiding something, though by the haughty expression on his face she imagines he thinks he is enacting some mystical silver service ritual. She bites her lip to hide a smirk.

'No, this will do.' The waiter almost bows and leaves. 'Pompous ass. Now to the business in hand. I've noticed, Ada – may I call you Ada?'

She nods, sawing through a pad of gristle and fat.

'Well, let me put it this way. We all know that Mr. Miller, poor chap, hasn't quite been himself lately. I don't want to be indiscreet, but it's hardly a secret that he hasn't been well for some time.'

Mr. Miller is the accountant of the firm. He is also her direct boss and, since his wife died, a drunk, and horribly incompetent. She chews slowly, saying nothing.

'And yet somehow, Ada, his work is done. The accounts are filed, various expenses have been authorised, his correspondence is in order. In fact, the books haven't looked better in some time. I was wondering if you could tell me how that is?' He stabs at a lump of meat and pushes it into his mouth, chews quickly and swallows it down like a snake swallows a whole sheep. He eats as if he is ravenous and suspects that someone will steal his food. She has noticed this about the English, how impulsive and base they can be.

'I'm not sure what you mean.' She places her cutlery on her plate and folds her hands in her lap. She presses her lips together, to quell the excitement that threatens to expose her.

'Oh come on, Ada. It's obvious to us, to me at least, that we owe you our thanks.'

'I don't think so, Mr. Robson.' It's much better, she thinks, to stay calm and humble. Not to brag about how a couple of months working for Mr Miller, sitting outside his office and listening to his meetings and calls, a day or two reading through the books and files was enough to for her to learn the job. She'd typed enough of his correspondence to know his particular ways and expression, it's really all very simple and fun and she'd been so bored. Not to mention she feels very sorry for Mr Miller who just can't seem to pull himself together.

'Now don't be coy, it's a waste of time. I take it was you who put our pulp supply out to tender?' He purses his lips in irritation and the bristles of his moustache protrude like the spines of a porcupine.

'Yes. Yes it was.'

'Congratulations, you've cut our costs by—'

'Twelve and half percent.' She clears her throat.

'Very good. Well, we've spoken to Mr Miller and he has decided, sensibly I think you'll agree, to retire.' He places his knife and fork on the table and steeples his hands, elbows on the table. Ada tries to ignore his junglee ways. 'So we are looking to replace him.'

She presses her hands against her thighs. Her breath is shallow and gathers at the base of her throat. The waiter appears and collects their plates, laboriously piling up their cutlery. She glares at him, hoping to hurry him along.

'Would you like the dessert menu, Sir?'

'No, thank you. Just the bill.' Finally the waiter leaves, his shoes scuffing against the faded carpet.

'You've done well, that's obvious, that's why this is such a shame. It just doesn't do, you see. If only you were a man, I'd give you the position in a flash, but you aren't and it doesn't instil confidence in the other staff if a slip of a girl is running rings around the management. It causes all sorts of problems. So I'm afraid you will have to join the other clerical staff.'

'I don't understand.'

'I'll see to it that you won't take a pay cut, not at all. We just think it's best if you work with the other girls in the typing pool. I think you'll enjoy it: much more fun.'

'This isn't fair. I'm more than able, you just admitted as much.' The collar of her blouse feels much too tight.

'Be that as it may, you also lied for him, you lied to us and jeopardised the company and your own position, by doing work you just aren't capable of.'

'But you said the books looked better than they had in a long time.' She suddenly feels ill, as if her stomach will turn inside out; a lump bulges in her throat. She closes her eyes for moment and swallows hard, placing her hands flat on the table to steady herself; the paper covering sticks to her damp palms.

'Yes, but for all we know that's just dumb luck, isn't it? Now look, don't be upset, a girl that looks like you should let men do all the work anyway.' He leans forward and places his hand on the table, his little finger – circled by a thick gold signet ring – very close to hers.

'I'm not upset, John, do you mind if I call you John?'

He smirks and gives a shocked, rather silly little laugh. He shakes his head and opens his mouth to speak, but she doesn't give him the chance.

'I'm not upset, John, I'm furious. With myself mostly, for being such a fool. I don't want your silly job, but I do want compensation.' She pulls her hand off the table and reaches for her handbag, tucked neatly against her chair leg.

'Now look here, Miss Kelly, I am fully within my rights to make these adjustments.'

'Perhaps you are. In fact, I don't doubt you are, but it would only be fair if you paid me for the work you admit I have done. At the very least. I don't expect an answer now, tomorrow will be fine.' She stands, sliding out from the table and drops her napkin on the chair. She doesn't rush, she doesn't fumble. She holds out her hand and shocked, he takes it.

She leaves, her head up, willing herself to the door without mishap.

TAMARA

Is her mother really sick? Is this a trick? A conspiracy? Perhaps a lure to get Tamara back home where her mother can kill her. Or weep and cry and apologise so that she has to forgive her, has to love her mother again, let her guard down, leaving herself vulnerable. Can you trust a doctor? She's not sure, as she is rarely ill, tries very hard not to be, was never allowed to be: a cut or break or fever was always met with impatience, or disbelief or resentment. A wide, puckered and grainy scar on her left bum-cheek bears witness to her mother being too busy for the hospital, for the inconvenience of stitches. Too busy getting ready for her new boyfriend to do anything more than pull out the fragment of glass, douse it in Germolene and cover it with a plaster. Silly little brat should know better than to run around outside.

Recently, when she couldn't ignore the angry hot raw skin that ached to be scratched and bled when she did rake her nails across it, the doctor, local, busy and kind, gently cupped her elbow and pressed cool tips of fingers against her flesh. She had to blink away idiot tears; it felt so good, so comforting to be touched. Not sexual, not a wanting anything kind of touch, not approval or forgiveness just confirmation she is there. She is so lonely. We remember that, the attention of doctors, the confirmation of being. The loneliness.

She's seeing a neurologist. They examine her head, sliding her into a tube to scrutinise the nerves. She suffers with her nerves, like us but not, this is different. She's not mad, not yet, it's just that her body has changed its relationship with the earth, with gravity and light. She has started to fall, stumble and trip, the ground sways and slips. The air and its gaseous concoction fizzes and prickles against her skin, light beams enter her eye in smart flashes. It feels like an undoing. Her body is a shaky vessel. Something wrong with her brain has altered time, slowed, changed her focus.

Not the same as before, that family sickness. The madness of women, trapped and raging and muzzled like beasts. No wonder they are crazy. We were crazy. Silenced and hobbled, made stupid and dumb. Our horizons snipped small. Only once for her, but never again. Never again the drug queue and the group therapy and the chain-smoked fags and art classes. Too tempting to stay. Warm and cared for. This sickness is different. Hands and feet slowly losing contact, disengaged from the outside world. Painful memory slips, eyes seeing an alternate reality. The shadows of something coming. The other side. Time multiplying. Floaters, small gaps in vision, as if the world is disappearing in fragments. Can she trust the doctors?

She is a translation. A bad one. The code has been perverted. It will, having been replicated too many times.

We taught her:
Matthew, Mark, Luke and John
Bless the bed that I lay on
Four corners to my bed
Four angels round my head
One to watch and one to pray and two to bear my soul away.

She took that to mean she would die in her sleep, silly girl. It was to keep her safe. To protect her. We didn't realise she wanted to die in her sleep.

CLAIRE

She ain't one to turn her nose up to a kindness, God knows she ain't got the right, but the bedsitting room Bert's got her makes home look like a palace. The shared loo in the hall stinks, the kitchenette is an electric ring too small to boil an egg on, with a stained sink and bucket to wash in, and because it's right by the docks the other tenants all seem to be working girls and their customers, a right rough lot. But, the bed's not too bad and it's all her own till Den gets his leave and everyone keeps to themselves pretty much and minds their own and, even though she's very busy with visitors, the girl next door seems nice.

Bless her Bert, she don't know where she'd be without him and his soft heart. He's managed to get some of the money and letters Den sent off their parents and has even bought her a pram, it's only second hand, but with a good scrub has come up nice. Her dad says she's dead to them now, but her mother sent over a matinee jacket and bonnet she knitted and a plaster statue of St. Francis, a pale dove perched on his lumpy hand. The old man still won't give her permission to get married; he says it's her punishment to live in sin like the slut she is with her bastard till she's twenty-one. He thinks Den will give up on her, and she'll have to come grovelling back. Over her dead body.

When the labour starts she's alone in her room scrubbing the skirting and the lino and it's lucky that Maureen, the girl next door, is in with a fella, cos she sends him out to the phone box to call a midwife and then stays with her while they wait. She's had a couple of her own though you couldn't tell, she's such a slip of a thing.

'There's nothing to it,' she says. 'Just let mother nature do the work.'

Funny how you're taught that some people, like working girls, are dirty and not like other decent folk, and yet here she is with a bun in the oven and no ring on her finger and relying on a kindness that is as gentle and clean and properly given as any she's ever had; and she herself as honest as she's always been and yet it's them that's fallen, them that's in the gutter.

The midwife arrives, all starch and snark, but she's glad of her coming because even though she knows female animals do this all the time, she's scared and she wants her mum and Christ it's harder than she imagined, harder than it looks, the contractions crushing the life out of her, and when her waters go with a great splash she thinks she'll lose her head the pains get so wild. She's gripping Maureen's hand so hard and roaring her head off and she might as well be an animal she's sunk so far in herself, into the pounding of her blood and the tearing apart of her body that she can't even think like a person, can't hear the words the midwife is saying and then just like that it's over and there's a relief and a cry and a slimy baby on her chest, a boy, a son, hers, and then there's a panic and the midwife still down there between her legs says there's another one and it all starts again, the gritting and clenching and pushing, and out comes another one. Twins. Two beautiful, healthy, identical boys. She's a mother and nothing else matters. Hasn't she achieved her life's holy account? Isn't this her purpose? But two. Two of them.

ADA

'When I was a girl,' her mother tells her, 'we understood our duty. Our duty to God, our duty to our parents, and our duty to ourselves.'

Ada stretches her legs out on the settee, rubbing her heels on the rough fabric and pointing her toes. The Virgin Mary looks down at her from a shelf in the alcove, sorrowful and as disappointed as her mother. She wiggles her toes for effect; she has become quite the dab hand at painting her nails.

'You barely come to Mass.'

'Mother, I come every Sunday.'

'Well, you have your mind on other things, I can tell you aren't paying attention, you make no room in your heart for God. You have no humility.'

'You can't possibly know what's in my heart, Mother.'

'You haven't found a new job, you just sit around here, doing nothing.'

'I have a job, remember, I start next week. Besides, I help you don't I?'

'You are brazen, you think you are capable of existing in the world of men and not losing out. Look at you! Painted toes, painted face, new clothes, doing a man's job and thinking it would be nothing. Of course they would sack you and without proper notice or pay. You have ideas above your station.'

'You made me work. I wanted to study, I wanted to go to university. But you made me go to that stupid secretarial school, all bloody bugger tippy tappy yes sir no sir and now this is what you get.'

'You will not learn will you? To bring shame on your family is to place a snake at its heart.'

'And what shame have I brought, Mother? What? I do your bidding, I keep quiet. I give you my keep. I clean and cook. What else do you want?'

'Why are you shouting?' Lilian, dressed in a thin organdie dress suitable for a little girl, tiptoes in on bare feet.

'Have you been in the garden without a hat?'

'I was sitting in the shade, Mother. I promise.'

Their mother squints at her face, examining her skin. 'I hope so, you know how the sun, even here, will ruin your complexion.'

'I know. So what were you screaming about? I think the whole street heard you.'

'Mother thinks I've brought shame on the family. I am such a terrible girl, you'd think I was the one who assassinated Gandhiji or something.'

'Don't you dare be so flippant. I'll bloody jhaap you, shameless girl.' Her mother steps closer, her arm raised as if to slap Ada, who doesn't even flinch. Her mother drops her hand, and stares at her daughters, breathing though her mouth. A little bubble of spittle glimmers on her top lip. She is powerless now. She has been erased by this country, by these girls, this life.

Lilian perches on the arm of the settee. 'I'll take a ringside seat if you're going give her a thrashing, Mummy.' She laughs, pinching Ada's little toe. 'Will you do mine for me?'

'Oh God, help me!' Their mother turns and rushes upstairs to her bedroom. They count, 'five, four, three, two, one,' and the door slams above them.

'You shouldn't upset her like that; you know how unhappy she is.'

'That's easy for you to say, just wait till you've finished classes and have to get a job. It's demeaning pretending to be stupid and to not mind the pats and stares and pinches.'

'Get married then. Find a husband, then you will be your own mistress, with your own house and all that business.'

'There has to be more to life than that, Lilian.'

CLAIRE

She's married now and in her own flat, one of the new council ones with its own bathroom and two bedrooms. They're on the list for an house, but till then this will more than do. She keeps it clean as a whistle, not a speck of dust. Minds her pennies, makes ends meet. Mistress of her own home. Her dad didn't stand a chance against her Den, one short visit and a few words in his ear and she had permission to wed just like that. Good job too, the registrar said it was a cruel thing to deny a girl and her babies legitimacy. Bert said Dad was ever so quiet after Den had been, he said Den was a sight to behold, not taking no for an answer; but she's dead to them now, her and the little 'uns, not to be spoken of in his house. She's best off out of it, she knows that, but it hurts so much she has to bite her lip to stop herself from crying. At least her boys need her and love her, their little eyes following her every move as she knits and cooks and cleans, smiling and babbling away on their blanket, never out of her sight.

Shirley pops in every now and then after she's finished school. She's doing her Pitmans, typing and shorthand; she's smart and every inch the little lady. And though a tiny part of Claire is jealous, she looks at her boys and the feeling is drowned by her love. Her new mother-in-law still ain't visited but it's all right, soon Den will be done with his service and home with them. They'll be a proper family and she won't be so lonely, especially with the next baby on the way, not twins this time, thank God, or so the midwife says. Mrs Shepherd she calls her, and how right and how good that sounds, sitting in the new clinic waiting room, her boys in their pram, her wedding ring closing off all gossip, all shame, standing up and gathering herself when they call 'Mrs Shepherd'. It's even better when the midwife pops the boys in the scales and weighs them like spuds and tests their hearing and their grip and how well they hold up their little heads and tells her what a marvellous job she's doing. There's a word for you, *marvellous*. Don't it fill your mouth like a sweet heavy cream?

TAMARA

She has had lovers, she's not defective. It's just the age-old problem, for some of us – you speak for yourself – enduring the grunting, thrusting, push-pull of men and their needs. Some of us could never get enough. Some of us had too much. Some of us had just what we wanted and needed.

'Have you heard from Christopher?'

'No, thankfully, nothing since the divorce, not even a nasty text message.'

'I heard he was seeing someone, a woman from his office. Toby saw a photo on Facebook.'

'Good luck to her, poor thing.'

'You're not bothered?'

'Why would I be?'

'I don't know, I wondered if you missed him sometimes?'

'God no, not at all.'

She is sitting on the polished wood floor of Pav and Toby's new flat. Toby is out for the evening, leaving them to drink beer, get stoned and eat Pav's mum's left-over Kitchri straight from the fridge.

'Not even the sex?'

'Definitely not the sex. I feel sick thinking about it.'

'This is too dry, sorry.' Pav pushes her bowl away. 'I'll order a pizza.' She swipes across her phone till she finds the right app and taps in the usual order. 'Done.'

'Can I grab another beer?'

'Help yourself. Get me one while you're there.'

She navigates around a stack of boxes to reach the fridge, pulling two cold bottles from the rack. The light pulses. She blinks, hard, and the pulsing stops. Her fingertips buzz and the walls tilt. She tells herself she is just stoned and goes back to the living room and Pav.

'Cheers, babe. So have you thought about getting back out there? You could get on Tinder, get yourself laid at least.'

Tamara laughs. 'You make it sound so romantic.'

'Who needs romance? You need some cock.' Pav wraps her lips around her beer bottle like it's a penis. Tamara laughs so hard she snorts beer.

'You're an idiot. Look at the state of me!' She rubs the front of her T-shirt with the flat of her hand.

'I'm serious though. You need some fun, you need a man, you're going to dry up like this old rice if you don't get out there.'

'Oh my God, listen to you! It's not the 1950s. I don't need a man, I'm happy as I am.'

'You know what I mean. There's nothing wrong with a bit of attention, a little loving, a few orgasms.'

'Stop yourself.'

'Let's get set you up on Tinder. Pass your phone over.'

'No, not now.'

'Oh, come on, it'll be a laugh.'

'No, seriously. I really don't want to.'

'All right, all right. Have it your way. But if I was single I'd be out there.' She leans forward, pulling a drag off her bong. It's an ironic bong, like something from the seventies. Orange tinted glass, smoky swirls in the bowl.

'You know what? I just don't miss any of it. If I want to hang out and have dinner, or whatever, I've got you and all my other friends. Or I can go out by myself. Honestly, it feels like having to put out and get fucked is too much of a price to pay for having some company.'

'What do you mean?'

'I mean, I don't care if I never have sex again. It just doesn't do it for me. It's a lot of mess and fuss for nothing. I'd rather read a book, or have a wank; at least you know what you're getting.'

'Really? But what about love? Being wanted?'

'I couldn't care less.'

'What's changed? You had plenty of boyfriends at Uni. Michael told Toby you were a right goer!'

'No he never! He didn't say that.'

'He did! I swear, he said you sucked his cock in a lecture.'

'That's disgusting. Anyway, I was just going along with it. Joining in with the whole being-a-student-and-fucking-around thing.'

'No, you weren't.'

'Yes I was. I was. I think I was just trying to be like everyone else.'

'That is weird and a bit sad.'

'Well, I'm over it now.'

'What about getting head?'

'God no, I feel exposed and under too much pressure: it's like, all that time and effort down there, you have to come for him. And what if you smell?'

'Oh Tamara, you're breaking my heart! You need to get some therapy.'

'I don't need therapy about sex. Maybe about everything else.'

'Perhaps it's men that are the problem.'

'Nope, I've slept with women. I just don't want sex, but everyone acts like it's the be all and end all.'

'It *is* the be all and end all. I love it. Getting close, skin on skin, licking and sucking and getting fucked and fucking him. I would be so sad if I couldn't fuck.'

'God, that sounds gross. Give me that.' She places her mouth on the bong and tries to light the weed, burning her fingers. Pav leans over and takes the lighter, expertly holding the flame to the bowl. Tamara doesn't feel close to her lover when she has sex: she feels confronted, used, pushed to the side. But she can't say that.

'That's it. Lightweight.' Pav takes a draw herself. Exhales. 'Look at the state of this place. I told Toby I'd finish unpacking. But I really can't be bothered.' She pushes a cardboard box an inch further away from her with her foot.

'I'd help you but I'm too stoned.'

'It can wait, Toby will do it eventually. You know what, I think I know what you are.'

'What do you mean?'

'I was reading an article a few days ago on some website about new sexualities and gender and stuff. You're what they call a hetero-romantic. That's what you are.'

'What?'

'Yep, you know... bi, homosexual, asexual, pansexual. You're attracted to men, so hetero, but you like all the stuff without the sex, so romantic. It makes sense. You need to find a bloke who's the same.'

'As if.'

'I bet they're out there. You just have to find one. There's probably a dating app out there that caters for exactly your problem.'

'Or not bother, and it's not a problem. I'm happy, I like my life. And I can't stand the idea of having to be fucked for the next however many years to have someone to eat dinner with and go to the cinema.'

She wants a cure, she wants peace, redemption, to be forgiven. We want obliteration, we want absolution, to be remembered; she wants to forget. To forget.

That's enough isn't it?

ADA

A dead horse blocks the street, its legs stiff, as if it is kicking at the air. The dark eyes blank and dull. Its tongue hangs untethered from its mouth. A cloud of flies has already gathered about its head. People stand and gawp while traffic builds up in both directions. The horse's owner is sitting on the kerb, his head hanging, still holding onto the lead rein as if the horse might suddenly bolt away.

'How do you think it died?'

'Over-worked, heart gave out most likely. There's no obvious injury.' Robert puts his arm around her and draws her away; she lets him. Though she's hardly the flimsy type, he seems to enjoy looking after her.

'Let's get a drink shall we? We could walk to the river, The Command House does a smashing lunch.'

'Why not?'

They pass a policeman, who looks barely old enough to be out of school, uneasy in his stiff uniform with its rows of shiny buttons and Robert calls out to him, 'Officer, there's a dead nag blocking the road up ahead.'

'Do I look like I'm from the knackers yard, Sir?'

'Well, someone needs to take charge, and it might as well be you.' His voices rings with authority, a calm expectation of obedience, and the bobby trots off towards the trouble, muttering under his breath. She tucks her hand in Robert's elbow, and he smiles down at her. He has good strong teeth. They have been courting now for a few weeks. She has met his family, and he hers. There's nothing particularly remarkable about Robert, in so much as he is clean, tall and athletic in an English way. He doesn't read a lot, but he is intelligent. He's been in the Navy and now is a young executive in the oil industry. He has potential, his own car, and he has good manners.

They sit outside the pub, looking out over the river as it opens out towards the sea. It is a military green with the smell of vegetal decay. A ship glides in towards the dockyard, smoke billowing from its funnel. They can just make out the shouts of the crew as they bring her in. A mob of seagulls gathers on the wall, waiting for scraps. She sips her gin and tonic, the ice numbing her lip.

'You really are very pretty,' he says, staring at her face as if he could eat her flesh clean off her skull. 'I could watch you all day.'

'Don't be silly.'

'I'm not. You're a goddess, a queen.'

'Is that so? Montaigne says, "On the highest throne in the world, we still sit only on our own bottom."'

'Does he now? See? Clever and gorgeous.'

'I'm not so clever, I've just read a little bit. I wish I'd read more, but my parents wouldn't let me go to university.'

'Wouldn't they? Why?'

'Because they don't think a woman should be educated, it would be a waste, apparently.'

'Nonsense. Anyone with the brains necessary should be allowed to study. Man or woman.'

She decides she will love Robert. If her parents won't let her take care of herself, then she can at least choose who she will marry; someone who will treat her like an equal.

'It doesn't matter now. Tell me about the Navy. Did you sail in a big ship like that one?'

'That one there is a frigate. I sailed on those and a huge battleship, not much call for them any more, though. Most of them have been scrapped.'

'A battleship? Aren't you too young for the war?'

'Yes, of course I am!' He laughs.

'Did you enjoy being a sailor? People say the most salacious things about them, you know. A girl in every port.'

'I've heard the rumours. I should be so lucky!'

She bats him on the arm and pokes out her tongue.

'Just kidding. It's hard work, but yes, I did. I liked travelling and seeing new places, when we docked, that is. I mean, a lot of the time it was the same old faces, day in day out.'

'I can imagine. I'd like to travel more. Where have you been?'

'Let's see: Malta, Sicily, Egypt, Africa. Canada. We saw these huge whales in the Atlantic, swimming alongside the ship. They were like islands rising up out of the sea.' He laughs at himself, blushing like a child. 'Listen to me! I sound like a silly girl.' He lifts his leg and rests his ankle on his knee; the sole of his perfectly polished shoe is thin and the heel worn down on one side, betraying his uneven gait, the roll of his ankle to one side. The only chink in his neat, shiny veneer.

'No you don't, you sound charming. I'd love to see a whale, I've seen river dolphins in the Ganges, and crocodiles of course, and elephants and tigers.'

'You've seen a tiger?' He sounds as if he doesn't believe her, his voice rising up the scale of incredulity.

'Yes, we almost didn't see it. We were driving on a narrow track and it was only because we had to reverse to let another vehicle pass that we saw it, lying in the shade. There was a snow leopard on our school wall once too, just perched up there flicking its tail like a common tabby.'

'You really are something, Ada. I've never met anyone like you.' He reaches over and takes her hand, stroking her palm with his thumb. He has a serious look on his face. Then a neat woman slides two plates on their table, breaking the spell.

'Two Ploughman's?'

'That's us.' Robert says, letting go of her hand and picking up his cutlery. He cuts into his wedge of damp-looking cheese and smears it with pickle.

'Do you miss India? It must have been some life in the Raj, I imagine.'

'Yes, it was.' This is the agreed story now: her father didn't just work for the Raj but was part of it, a pukkah English man. It's easier all round not to go into detail. 'But we're here now and we have to make the best of it.' She chews a piece of limp lettuce, washing it and part of herself down with a swig of her drink.

TAMARA

The illness – they say it's an illness, though it often feels like an act of spite – is handed down through the family like a tarnished heirloom. Like a virus, some kink in our DNA. Though usually unspoken, or at least unnamed and therefore silenced, it broods in the hollows of the mind. A distant father romanticised it, glorified its attributes, as if being touched by it lifted him from the ordinary. For many of our mothers, grandmothers, it was a sentence. An unravelling. One aunt said it was like second sight, that she knew and saw things the rest of us couldn't, but it killed even her eventually.

We watch for signs, moodiness, excessive energy, lethargy and impulsiveness with the vigilance bred from fear. We count the features we shared – bad teeth, a curved index finger and a large nose – and wonder if among those features was the thing, the illness. We remember feeling so tired of falling and wanting to hit the ground sooner rather than later. The mother's untiring cleaning, singing, building her children tents with sheets on the line, laughing, laughing till she cried and flirting with every man who crossed her path, these are signs. We just didn't know them then. Neither did we know that her angers, as sudden and mysterious as fish, or her week-long silences, or that her hungers, her swamping affection that covered us in her kisses, were too.

Tamara has a solution.

CLAIRE

Up even earlier than usual this morning, she has the house done and dusted, with a banana and walnut loaf in the oven before the boys even wake up. She's done her hair in a nice wave and is wearing a new frock in a lovely printed pique cotton that barely shows her bump. She's even got some new shoes. The boys look perfect in their matching little rompers side by side in their pram and are in a biddable mood, all smiles and coos and dribbly babbles. The warm loaf is wrapped in paper in her bag. She knows she shouldn't and she knows Den will go mad if he finds out, but she's taken to visiting her mother when her dad is out. She's seen her dad in the street, it'd be impossible not to in this bloody place, and he didn't say a word, couldn't even look her in the eye, all mouth and no trousers that miserable old sod, but best to avoid him anyway.

She knows Den's right to tell her to stay away from 'em, but she can't help it; somehow she misses 'em. It's lonely at home alone. She loves her babies but they ain't hardly big talkers now and sometimes she just wants a little natter and to get out of the flat. It don't matter that the last couple of times she did all her mother's ironing while Annie and June sat and gossiped what with little Maryann courting already; their mother sitting in the middle like an old queen. They half-whispered about women's troubles and who's under the doctor and what tablets they're on, even though there's no one around to hear them. Her sisters' kids were given glasses of orange squash and a biscuit and were allowed to play in the yard or were bounced on knees and clucked over, while hers were left in the hall in the pram, unnoticed. She give 'em sips of tea from her saucer and kissed their precious little heads herself.

They ain't forgiven her. Won't forgive her for all the upset and trouble she caused. She's ruined. She hears it in her bones, hears like a murmur deep in her marrow, but she tells herself that it takes time, that they'll come around eventually. Blood is thicker than water, and she's happy to listen and help out and the more they see how well she's doing the easier it will be. She has to try. No harm in trying and it'll all be forgotten about soon, old news. They'll accept her and the kids and Den and be happy for her. They're family.

Her new shoes are too tight and cutting into her heels something chronic, but she pushes on. Stops for a minute to catch her breath and shift her bag onto her other arm. 'Not much further now, my darlings.'

It's warm for October and her face is damp and if she ain't careful her hair will go limp but if she takes much longer the loaf will be cold and the boys will need a feed and start grumbling.

'Right, let's get a move on shall we?' She leans in and heaves them up the hill where her family's house squats at the end of the pebble-dashed terrace.

TAMARA

The chair is particularly uncomfortable. Moulded plastic screwed onto a steel frame, but warped with age and a multitude of bodies. The left side presses into her back, twisting her spine. She shifts from one buttock to the other. Tries to find the least painful position. Across from her the doctor is reading her notes on a screen. Notices and reminders and checklists printed on sheets of A4 paper, some more pristine than others, are tacked to the damp yellow wall behind his head. She wishes the doctor was female, but then it might not make a difference. She shifts again.

'So, you're here to discuss sterilisation, is that right?'

'Yes.'

The doctor pauses, scrutinising her face. He nods, as if agreeing with his own unspoken conclusion. 'You realise that it's permanent?'

'I do.'

'You're very young for such a drastic procedure.'

'I'm thirty.'

'Exactly. That's very young. What if you change your mind?'

'I won't.'

'What about your husband?'

'I'm divorced.'

'Right, I see. But what about in the future? You may marry again and your new husband want children. Then what?'

'Then he can have children.'

'But not with you.'

'Exactly, not with me. No.'

'Can I ask why you want this?'

She stares at a rota fixed just behind his right shoulder; someone has scrawled over the neat print in blue biro. 'Because the idea of becoming a mother terrifies me. I have my work, I have my life. I don't want children. The pill makes me ill, crazy. I've tried all the other methods and I just want it all done with. No risk. No messing around. Done and dusted.'

He sighs, 'OK, let's get your medical history and we'll go from there. Any pregnancies?'

'Yes, one.'

'What happened?'

'I had an abortion.'

'Right.' He makes a note. 'How long ago was that?'

'Not sure. Five years ago I think.'

'Contraception?'

'No, not at the moment. It's not necessary.'

He stops typing and looks at her, pursing his lips – she notices how full and pink they are, his skin soft and clean shaven – 'I will refer you to the surgeon for the procedure, but please think this through, you're very young. What if you change your mind? Being a mother is a gift, a joy...'

Her mother says, 'I've changed my name, I'm not Mum anymore.' She also says, 'Never have children, it's hell. Ruins your life. I wish you'd never been born.' She says, 'One day I'll leave you in the children's home and never come back.'

Tamara wants to say, 'Who the fuck do you think you are?' She wants to say, 'Fuck you. What makes you think I'd be a good mother? What makes you think every fucking woman wants a baby?'

She says, 'Thank you, doctor.'

ADA

The cloudy sky masks the sun as well as curtains would have, if they'd remembered to draw them last night before their tumble into bed. They have missed breakfast but what else is a honeymoon for but to lie in? Robert snores lightly next to her, laying on his back, one arm across his chest. She lifts the sheet a little peering in the soft half-dark at his body. The lumps of muscle on his arms, the freckled points of his elbows, his tender belly, the tough short hairs on his chest, the fragile curl of his penis. He is all hers. She reaches for her diary, she wants to remember everything.

Everything she had been told about her wedding day, and most especially her wedding night, had been wrong. Everyone made such a fuss about the ceremony and the satin gown and the lace and the church and the wedding breakfast as if that would be the crowning moment of her life, and yet she just felt like a doll on display, smiling and nodding and bored; performing a version of herself created especially for that day. The wedding night, on the other hand, was wonderful, despite all the warnings that it would be painful, and that she must bear it for the sake of her husband, to not worry if it was difficult. Instead, she feels as if she has been released from some subterranean place, raw-fleshed, nerves exposed, blinking hard in this new light. She writes: like Persephone free of the Underworld, she has emerged from the darkness of virginal ignorance into the glow of knowledge. She writes about being reborn in a tangle of limbs, breath and kisses. His skin on hers, the soft sheets and heavy blankets wrapped around them, caressing them, all sensation and belonging utterly to the moment. Just being, no pretence, no forged expression on her face. Just herself. How has she had this body for twenty-two years and not seen its beauty? Not felt its potential? All things she ought not to be thinking and feeling and wanting. But why not, when she has become so good at being someone else?

'Good morning. What's my bride up to?'

She shuts the diary, tucks it under her pillow and leans over to kiss him. 'Writing about how happy I am.'

'Are you happy?' His fingers graze the curl of her ear, follow the line of her neck and rest on her shoulder.

'Of course, I am.' She pulls back to look more closely at his face, worried that he needs to ask, but he grins, teasing.

'Prove it.' He pulls her on top of him, kissing her neck and breasts.

'We've missed breakfast.'

'Then I'll just have to eat you.'

A trolley rattles outside in the corridor accompanied by the scuffing of soft shoes on the carpet. The hotel runs according to schedule, even if its guests do not. Robert is drowsing again, recovering his power he calls it, as if she has drained him of some essential masculine energy. She, on the other hand, only feels more vitalised and replenished after they've finished; greedy for more. She dresses, pulling on a skirt and blouse, knotting a jersey around her shoulders. She glances out of the window; the lake is just visible between the tree-studded hills. She tugs on his left toe, surprised by the tuft of hair sprouting above the nail bed. She thought she'd explored all of his body, uncovered its secrets.

'Come on, Sleepy. Let's go for a walk.'

He groans and turns over, hiding his face in the pillow like a little boy before sitting up. 'Must we? Can't we just stay here?'

'No! Let's walk to the lake, have a cup of tea and a change of scene. The maid needs to change our linens anyway and she can't with you lying there, can she?'

'Why bother? We'll only mess them up again.' He pats the bed beside him. 'Come on in, Mrs Robert Hailsham, I need you.'

'Whilst your offer is very tempting *Mr* Robert Hailsham, I am starving and I must decline. However,' she pulls the sheet from his body and kisses his chest, 'if you'll accept these kisses as a down payment,' she kisses his stomach and the tip of his cock, 'I'll pay in full later.'

'Done.'

She combs her hair while he dresses, watching him in the mirror: the tightening lift of skin that slackens again, the light shifting the colour of his hair, the long, flat planes and angles of his clothed body, the alien routine of male garments. It is his resistance to her, his opposition to her femininity that she wants to consume. His neck and chin are red raw from where he shaved too quickly; a nick of tissue paper absorbs a spot of blood on his cheek. He ties his shoes, one foot then the other on the ottoman, unaware that he is performing for her.

She is curled into an armchair in the hotel lounge, her stockinged feet tucked under her skirt. She rearranges the cards in her hand, and watches as Robert discards the jack of diamonds, frowning. A white man, with flabby jowls and very short grey hair, brings them a glass of brandy each. He takes extra care not to disturb Ada's line of melds, the tidy piles of cards signalling her higher score. He smiles at them both, kindly and with a knowing look, as most people in the hotel do, from the chambermaid to the sprightly woman at the reception desk. She guesses it is a look they bestow on all newlyweds, especially the ones who miss mealtimes and look dazed and exhausted as she knows they do. Robert sucks on his drink and wipes his top lip. He doesn't look at her. She picks up the discarded jack and places it on the table along with the jack of hearts and the jack of clubs, tossing the five of diamonds onto the discard pile.

'Done!' Robert groans and throws his cards down.

'Shall I add the scores?'

'Don't bother, you've won by a mile.' He leans back in his seat and rests his drink against his cheek, stretching his legs out in front of him. His feet push the table between them towards her as if he is suddenly growing out of the original space he granted himself. He makes himself bigger. She picks up her glass and extends it towards him; he greets it with a clumsy clink and a muttered 'Cheers,' still not looking at her.

'What's my prize?' She smiles at him, leaning forward in her seat and resting her hand on his knee. 'Even beginners luck deserves a reward, doesn't it, Mr Hailsham?'

The jowly waiter moves about the room behind them, switching on table lamps and straightening cushions on the sofas. Robert huffs and pulls his legs in to sit up straight.

'Winning is its own reward.' He finishes his drink and puts the glass down on top of the score sheet; he pinches the bridge of his nose and closes his eyes.

'Don't sulk, darling, we had such a nice morning at the lake.' And they had, walking hand in hand around the lake shore, kissing on a bench overlooking the rocky islands – holms Robert called them, not islands, but still islands in the vast lake – watching the geese glide across the water, followed by tea and cake at Bowness. Even the weather had held for them.

'I'm not sulking, for God's sake, I'm not a child. I've got a headache.'

'Shall I get you something for it?'

'Ada, please. Will you stop? I don't need you to patronise me.' He stands and brushes the creases from his trousers. 'I'm just going out for some fresh air. I won't be long. I'll be back for dinner. Finish your drink.'

He leaves her, just like that, in a small hotel that until this moment she hadn't noticed reeked of the distilled musk of everything English – particles of damp, mould spores, lard, boiled vegetables, furniture polish and denture cream. She feels sick, her cheeks hot, and yet at the same time she doesn't really care.

CLAIRE

But she's happy. They've got four little ones now, two girls to balance the twins. She's got her house finally, with a front and back garden so she can grow flowers and fruit and have a vegetable patch. She sows lines of beans and peas and winds nets over raspberry and gooseberry bushes like she's wrapping up her hair after a shampoo and set. The kids have got a swing. They've got a telly off Radio Rentals, and she's got a lovely set of Pyrex dishes and a matching dinner service. The parlour is for best and she keeps it spotless; the front room is for every day, no visitor ever goes in there, and they've got three good sized bedrooms and a bathroom. They make ends meet and have a little bit left over. She has her hair done every week and she's kept her figure. She keeps to the standards set.

Den works hard and loves her, dotes on the kids, still makes her laugh. When he gets in from work he leaves his boots at the door and washes the grease and oil off his hands before grabbing her for a kiss and then cuddling the little 'uns. Hands over his wages every Friday, keeping only a bit for himself; rarely goes to the pub, never to the bookies. He's bought a car, the only one on the street, and tinkers with it every weekend to get it going again. It's a right old banger, but if it's got an engine he can fix it and it won't be long before they can pile the kids in the back and go on jaunts to the seaside and drives in the country. He's a good man, everyone says so, but still she checks his collar and his underpants for signs of other women, gets upset if he so much as glances at anyone on the street. She's never found nothing, but she knows what men are like, what they need, ain't they all the same? You can't be too careful and you can't be this happy without something taking it all away. Nothing this good can last. And she can't pretend she don't love being with him, next to him, under him; she can't pretend that he don't fill up a need in her that seems to open up the minute he's out the door, that she can't bear to lose him.

'You all right, girl?' Bert pops his head round the door and half scares the life out of her.

'Bloody hell, Bertie! You're like a cat burglar you are.'

'Sorry babe, didn't mean to scare you. Just dropping off some veg and bits, some nice plums in there an' all, just for you.' He dumps two paper sacks on her clean tops and dry mud scatters everywhere. She ignores it.

'I forgive you. Tea?'

'Go on then, I can spare five minutes for my favourite sister.'

'Give over, you charmer.' She lights the gas under the kettle and, with the same match, sparks up a fag from the pack on the counter. 'Want one?'

'Nah, you're all right. How you keeping then?' He parks himself on one of her new kitchen chairs.

'Yeah, we're fine thanks. And you?'

'I've got news.' He's grinning like the cat that's got the cream.

'Go on then.' She hands him his tea. 'Sugar's in the jar. What is it?'

'You better sit down.'

'Get on with it then, tell me.' She lifts rather than pulls the chair so as not to scratch her lino.

'I'm engaged! Lizzy said yes!'

'Oh Bert! I'm so happy for you. That's lovely news, really lovely.' She pats his hand before tapping her ash into the pot. 'When's the happy day? I shall have to get meself a hat.'

'We ain't set a date yet, and it'll just be a small do anyway. Nothing special. I think Lizzy wants to keep it small, you know her mother's been taken bad.' He finishes his tea in a wide gulp, his head tipped back, his young neck a patchy red from shaving.

114

'That makes sense, no point in wasting money on a big do, all that fuss and bother. I'll just have to wait till the first christening to go hat shopping.' She smiles and stubs out the fag. Puts a brave face on, because it won't do Bert any favours to see her upset and it's hardly his fault she's still not welcome in the family. Bless his heart, he never was any cop at fibbing and why should he be? 'You'll bring me round a bit of cake though, won't you? And show me the album?'

'Of course I will. I'm sorry, Claire, you know if I could change his mind I would.'

'Don't worry about it. I'm happy for you, this is lovely news, better than winning the pools. I better get on: the kiddies will be up from their sleep in a minute.'

'Right then, I'll be off. I'll bring Lizzy round soon, shall I?'

'You do that. I'll make a nice tea for us.'

'Smashing.' He gets up to go and is only one foot out the door before he turns back. 'Here, have you heard about Mum?'

'Heard what?'

'She's only up the duff again, and at her age!'

'She ain't!'

'She is. That's a turn-up, ain't it? See you later then.'

She stays sitting for a minute, waiting to hear the gate clang shut behind him before biting into the flesh at the top of her arm so hard that the blood wells under the surface there and then. She lights a fag, her hands shaking. Upstairs the kids are stirring: she can hear the boys bouncing on their beds. In a minute the baby will cry and it'll be bedlam but she takes a deep drag, filling the dark hollows of herself with smoke.

Annie had opened the door, keeping one shoulder braced behind it. 'You have to go, you can't come in.'

'What d'you mean, I can't come in?'

'You have to leave, now. Dad found out you've been round and there's been bloody murders all week.'

'But I've made a cake and everything.'

Annie just looked at her, her mouth pressed tight.

'Can I speak to Mum, at least?'

'She don't want you here neither. Not you or your kids. Now go before he comes back and sees you. I mean it. Don't come here.' Annie shut the door.

She walked home barefoot, the bloody shoes in her bag, the skin on her heels raw and bleeding. She didn't cry though, she weren't going to give them the satisfaction, and even though it stuck in her throat she ate every last bit of that banana and walnut loaf. She'd show 'em, the nasty gits. She'd show the lot of 'em.

TAMARA

Bathed, hair washed with no stingy soap in her eyes, nightie and dressing gown on, cuddling her ragdoll, Polly. Sitting on nanna's lap, who is sitting on the floor between grandad's legs, who is sitting in his chair. The electric fire is on, all three bars burning red hot. Grandad is peeling oranges, carefully removing all the pith and pips and handing the segments to his girls. They're all sucking on the sweet juice of the orange – perfectly segmented, no bitter skin or stringy bits. They're watching Eric and Ernie. They're laughing. The little girl is happy. This is all she knows for now.

She found a 50p in the jar for the leccie meter, made herself a jam sandwich and is eating it on the sofa watching EastEnders. She kicks off her sandals and flexes her toes, dares to put her feet up on the glass coffee table. Licks jam from her fingers and then wipes them on the arm of the sofa. The front door opens and she sits up straight, feet on the floor, covers the arm of the sofa with her elbow. Her mum comes in, alone, not drunk exactly, but happy to see her. She pulls a bottle out from her bag and waggles it at her. 'Want a glass?'

'I'm not allowed, Mum.'

'Oh go on, don't let me drink on me own. One won't hurt you, besides, you should learn how to drink at home, where you're safe. Just one, with your mother.' She goes out to the kitchen and Tamara checks for breadcrumbs and marks from her feet on the table. She rubs the glass with the hem of her T-shirt, just in case.

Her mother comes back in with two glasses of wine and hands one over; it has ice cubes in it on account of her being twelve. They clink cheers and Tamara takes a sip. It's not that bad. Her mother's eyes are droopy, like she's almost asleep. 'I love you so much, my babe. So much. You know that, right?'

Tamara nods.

'Good girl. You're a good girl. I was just saying to Beverly, you remember my friend, Bev? The big girl?' Tamara nods and so she goes on: 'I said to her, who needs a man when you've got kids already? That's real love, that's all you need. I was telling her how proud I am of you.' She pauses to drink and swallow. She licks her lips and her head wobbles, like her moving tongue threw it off balance. 'I just want you to be happy. That's all. I'm not perfect, but I want you to be happy.' She starts to cry, her face screwed up like a paper ball. 'So happy, not like me. I said to Bev, you can't trust men. None of 'em. Not a single one. Not even your own family. Look at what my brother did to me! My own brother. My flesh and blood, but I'll tell 'em one day. I'll get my own back. Mark my words. Fucking men. Don't ever trust a man, babe. Promise me. Promise me?'

The girl nods again, the rest of her body stiff, waiting for what comes next. Her ears ring. She already knows who she can and can't trust. Her mother finishes her drink, still crying, and lays her head down on the girl's lap. Unsure what to do, the girl strokes her mother's hair back from her sweaty face. Her mother's lips are parted, letting a thread of drool trickle down the girl's leg. Her mother snores, the empty glass still in her hand. Someone knocks on the door, and then knocks again, harder and for a few seconds longer than is polite. She hears the hinge of the letter box squeak.

'It's Mrs Bailey, Provident lady. Hello?'

There's a pause, and Tamara knows the woman is listening at the door because there is no return squeak of the letter box.

'Is anyone home? I've come for this week's payment. Hello.'

There's the squeak and a final knock on the door. Tamara imagines her standing out there, frowning, licking the lead of her pencil to write in her notebook. Her nan says you get poisoned from licking your pencil. Here's hoping. Whenever she sees Mrs Bailey on the street she looks at Tamara like she's dirt. We know the type, smug, prissy and too happy to pick the flesh off the bone to make a profit. The type that squints her eyes to save a smile. We've got her number.

Tamara waits, her legs going numb, keeps watching the telly. The woman goes away and her mother doesn't wake.

Her best friend teaches her to use tampons; it's about time. The thick sanitary towels bulge in her underpants and make her waddle, they're uncomfortable and they stink. That's if her mother remembers to buy her the sanitary towels. Even worse is wads of tissue shoved in her knickers that don't stay put.

Michelle is in the cubicle next to hers, calling out instructions. She does as she's told. Puts one foot up on the toilet, bends her knees. Slides the cardboard cylinder inside herself, presses the plunger. Wraps the cardboard tube in tissue and flushes it. Straightens her clothes, washes her hands. It doesn't hurt, in fact she can't feel a thing. She's a woman now, truly. Honestly. Michelle has given her a couple of old bras too. She is wearing one of them now.

She hides the tampons in her room, tucking them behind books on her shelf, but when she comes down for dinner her mother puts them in front of her plate. She blushes and grabs them off the table, hiding them in her lap.

'So that's your virginity gone then, you dirty slut. If you think I'm buying them for you, think again. You can bleed all over yourself.'

This dad shakes his head at her mother. 'Hey, don't embarrass the poor kid.'

'Stay out of it. You don't know what she's like.'

It's a shame, he is a good one, teaches her how to punch properly, keeping her elbows in and her guard up, how to plant her feet and how to protect herself in a knife fight. She forgets everything he shows her but she cries when he leaves and doesn't come back. Her mother accuses her of fucking him.

Just on the periphery, at the edge of vision just beyond what can be seen clearly or sensed. But still, there, if only the lingering after-light of movement, the disturbance of molecules. The permeable boundaries of past present and future leaking and mixing and contaminating. Distorting.

But she will purify. Final act. She has stopped the future. Cut it off. Like a wart, twisted at the root, its blood supply stopped so it will wither and dry off. All that's left is the past, and that only requires one quick motion. The flick of a switch. And then she is pure. Innocent. Untethered.

CLAIRE

Baby after baby, but he won't leave off her, loves her too much and how can she deny him? If you don't give a man what he wants, what he needs, he'll go elsewhere. But baby after baby, something in her is wearing thin, she's tired, pale, too skinny; even the doctor says too much Mrs, too much, like it's her fault, like she's got a choice. But how else will she keep him, how else will she make sure he's hers? We can help the doctor says, but it ain't cheap, ain't on the National Health, and Den wouldn't like it. He provides for 'em all, don't he? Even though each time, each baby, her nerves get worse and the carrying on gets harder, the crying the cleaning and the watching. She can't stop. Slave to them all. Endless work. But how she loves them, their little hands curled around her finger. All that love that belongs to her. Every baby a blessing, so precious and she wouldn't give 'em up for the world, but a rest would be nice.

She feels everyone watching – her mother, her sisters, the neighbours; the sly looks they give her when she passes them in the street, ain't you got no pride? Her mother's one to talk, the old cow, eleven kids and the youngest the same age as her grandchildren. How dare they judge her? The babes and house are as clean as a whistle, she runs up new clothes for 'em all on her Singer, they're well fed, they're in school and every Christmas they get a toy, a chocolate bar and an orange. God help her, she won't tell them nasty cows how much she hurts sometimes because really she's happy, she knows she is. This is what she always wanted, ain't it?

ADA

Ada is exhausted. Her legs are like jelly, her arms too tired to raise herself. She lies back, her eyes closed. In the room others move around her. She hears their muted voices, the swish of fabrics, the bell clang of metal instruments being rinsed and dropped onto a tray. Someone, she's too tired to open her eyes to see whom, wipes her face and neck with a cool wash cloth. She smells lavender and a stiffer, astringent scent just under the floral. Detergent. Purifying. Perhaps she sleeps for a bit, a few minutes, possibly more. She hears a male voice, not her husband or father, confirming she doesn't need stitches, just as several female voices had already said. Then she is nudged, gently at first, then more firmly. 'Miss? Miss? It's time to wake up. Come on now, mother, you must wake up'. She rouses, her head spinning, eyes heavy as if brass coins still weighted them for the boatman, and there before her, taking slow, rheumy shape, is a midwife, starched and proper. Uncannily, but politely, clean of blood or shit or amniotic fluid, considering. She is holding out a woollen wrapped parcel, no, a baby. Yes, a baby parcel, wrapped in a woollen blanket, its little head protruding. She holds the baby out, waiting for Ada to take it, proffers the child, eyebrow raised. A question? She reaches out, still weak, and the midwife steps forward and tucks the baby parcel into her arms. That's that then. She is a mother. The child has light skin, fair hair.

CLAIRE

Day in, day out. Up before the lot of 'em. Electric fire on, bowl of water to wash in, bathroom too cold to strip down. Get the breakfast on, porridge for the kiddies, bacon butty for Den. Make him a cheese and pickle sandwich for his packing up, a boiled egg. See him off with a kiss and wish she could swap places with him, just for a day perhaps. Get 'em up, feed 'em, wash 'em, dress 'em. Get the older ones off to school. Get the little ones ready for shopping. Baby Josie in the pram, little cheeks flushed and grizzling what with her cutting her teeth and always hard to settle anyway; Vanessa, her reins tied to the pram, cos the little tomboy's always trying to pull away; and Gayle, prettiest of the lot but always wanting a cuddle, always needing something, perched on the pram seat sucking her thumb. Off they go, down to the shops getting her fruit and veg from Mr Bailey, though his produce ain't as good as her dad's, but beggars can't be choosers and there's no point worrying about it. A pound of mince and some chops from the butcher, the miserable old sod; milk powder, flour, eggs, lemon juice, tin of spam and digestive biscuits from the corner shop and 4 yards of red gingham, bias binding, thread, a tube of white buttons and ten ounces of pink wool from the haberdasher for the girl's summer dresses and cardies. Nice little chat with Peg, whose got her own little lot now, all girls so far and as sweet natured as their mother, with her curls too; but not too long because there's dinner to fetch and the washing to do and a tidy up before getting tea on and Den and the other kids get in.

There's the getting in and unpacking and putting away before feeding again; bread and jam will do 'em, including herself, and leaving the baby in the pram for some air she puts the other two down for a sleep. Cup of tea and a fag, then soaking her monthly rags in a bucket to water the garden, a witches' trick her dad used to say; boiling up left-over fish bones, carrot tops, onion for stock; melting down corners of soap and making new; tea leaves on the garden; just a corner of chocolate for a treat, make it last, make do, hands that keep busy. Always known how, sister, daughter, mother, wife, a dab hand before she's out of nappies herself.

All the knowing and wisdom, the habits and curses. Superstitions and protections, charms and jinxes. Crossing a baby's palm with silver. God bless. Pulling the curtains on a storm, opening the front and back doors to let it through, mind you. Turning the mirrors and opening the window after a death to let the soul out without a scare. Don't cast a clout till May is out. Too much of anything is bad, even if it's good; a fire needs oxygen but too much blows it out. Red sky at night, shepherd's delight, a warning in the morning. Keep yourself to yourself and never let 'em see your hurts. If there's bad luck hanging about sweep up a storm through the house and sweep out the bad from the back and the front doors, knock the broom on the threshold three times and then mop the floor with rose water. That'll cure what ails you. Count the magpies: one for sorrow, two for joy, three for a girl, four for a boy, five for silver, six for gold, seven for a secret never to be told. The rich are filthy and will live like pigs if you let 'em. Matthew Mark Luke and John, bless the bed that I lay on. Never lend what you can't afford to give. Mary Ann, bread and jam, marmalade and treacle; bit for you, bit for me, bit for all the people. Hail Mary, full of grace, Blessed is the fruit. A bit of how's your father, slap and tickle. Red brick, pebble dash, chicken wire, paving stones. Sticks and stones might break your bones but words will never hurt you. Liar, liar pants on fire. Girls in green should never be seen, red shoes no knickers, where there's muck there's brass, who does she think she is? The priest is no use, mealy mouthed, dry old git. All mouth and no trousers, pride comes before a fall. I speak as I find, and if you don't like it you know what you can do.

Peeling potatoes with the bowl between her legs, watching the kiddies playing, Josie chewing on a rusk. Feeding the washing, heavy as a sack of puppies, through the mangle. Pegging it out and hoping it don't rain. Rolling out the pastry, trick to it is having cold hands. What's that they say? Cold hands, warm heart. Ice inside the windows and coats on top of blankets, hot water bottles and eventually the electric blanket. Body aching, either the curse or a baby, bosom heavy with milk, nipples cracked and sore till they harden up, toughen. Hands the same. Heart the same. Toughening, hardening. Day in, day out.

ADA

Ada drifts from the sitting room to the dining room, past small gossipy groups standing in corners or perched on industrial-looking furniture, women in full skirts wielding martinis, men in uncomfortable-looking suits. This is her husband's new world, these people. Her sharp shoes sink into the thick carpeting. She leans against a large teak sideboard, her hip pressing against the curved edge. A heavy glass ashtray, more decorative than useful, and a matching vase empty of flowers sit on the sideboard in perfect symmetry. A painting, abstract blocks of yellow and red intersected by straight black lines, hangs above a marble fireplace that is the only original feature left in the house. The dining set is brand new too, a complicated system of glass and plastic and metal to seat eight people. There isn't much upholstery or cushioning anywhere in the house, as if the owners are penitents, abstaining from warmth and softness. Robert says that with one more promotion they will have a house like this, too. They already have a semi-detached three bedroom with a garage, bought with a mortgage; she has her own little car, much to the disapproval of her parents; there are fitted wardrobes in the bedrooms; she has a large fridge, a washing machine, a new three piece suite. She doesn't see why they should need more, especially as another promotion would mean even more time left alone with her boredom while he works to buy all these things. Things that confirm their place in the world. Things that further divide him from her, cluttering up the space between them.

Last night he turned away from her again. 'Too tired' he said, his body unresponsive. His broad shoulders blank and unbroachable. She suspects there is another woman but won't lower herself to ask. Lilian, who is married now with small children of her own, thinks it's up to the woman to control the situation, that if goes wrong then you can only blame yourself. 'What more do you want?' she asked, leaning back against Ada's sofa, her coffee cup perched on her pregnant belly. 'You've got everything. What else can you possibly need? All his attention? He's only a man.' She's not sure what she wants, but she wants more. She is bored, so bored, she can feel her mind shrivelling up, the world shrinking to her narrow routines. She has become provisional, mutable depending on her situation. No one in her own right, only recognisable as an appendage.

'I love your trousers, very modern, very beatnik.'

'What? Yes, thank you. I'm sorry, I was lost in thought.' Ada smooths the waistband of her silk cigarette pants.

'I could tell. I'm Susan.' The woman holds out her hand and presses Ada's, not so much a shake as a cursory touch. Older than Ada, her make up settling into the lines and creases around her eyes, she has a boldness, a way of looking at a person that seems to see straight through them. 'You must be the wife of my husband's new wunderkind.'

'Ada.'

'Nice to finally meet you, Ada. I've heard a lot about you.'

'Have you?'

'Yes, Robert is quite smitten with his bride and I can see why.'

'Thank you.' Susan continues gazing at Ada, a thin smile on her lips. Ada feels the colour rising on her cheeks.

'You have a lovely home.'

'Do you think so? I'm not so sure, it seems a little austere. Still I can always change it again. I'm always in need of a project, something to get my teeth into. It all gets very dull otherwise. You have children?'

'Yes, a boy and girl.' She thinks of them tucked up at home, blue-eyed and fair-skinned despite the sly comments from her in-laws about half-caste babies.

'What age are they?'

'Our daughter is three and our son almost two.'

'Heavens, so close in age! You do have your hands full.'

'Yes, it was an adjustment. Each child changes the composition of the family, doesn't it? Like chemical compounds altering a pH balance.' The woman frowns, her lips pursed around her cigarette. Ada changes tack: 'Yes, they're a handful.' The woman draws on her cigarette with something like relief.

'I remember how relentlessly monotonous it can be.' She exhales two flurries of smoke from her nose, one arm clutching her waist, the other bent at the elbow, the hand circling, the cigarette twirling and punctuating the air like a majorette's baton. She adds, 'But worth it, of course.'

'Of course. I should find my husband. You haven't seen him have you?'

The woman reaches behind Ada and grinds out her cigarette in the heavy glass bowl. 'Robert? I last saw him holding court outside with the other boys.'

Sliding the heavy glass door open she hears Robert's voice: 'What the wife doesn't know can't hurt her, and anyway, a man with steak at home sometimes needs plain cornflakes for the change!' Greeted by a swell of male laughter. She steps down on the paving stones and into the lamplight.

'Speaking of beloved wives!' Robert steps forward and kisses her cheek. 'Here's mine. This is Ada. Darling, I'd like you to meet Colin, my boss.' She shakes the hand of a large, ruddy-cheeked man. 'This is Jim, he keeps us on our toes.' A tall, thin man stands up and grasps her hand in both of his and presses it hard. 'And these other scoundrels are Nigel and Paul.' She nods and smiles, sitting in Robert's vacated seat. He stands behind her, his hand resting on her shoulder.

'Here you all are!' Two other women join them. The men stand and give them their seats amid a polite flurry of introductions and cigarette lighting, the smoothing of skirts and trouser creases. Ada gazes out at the garden as a tiny bat flits over the neat lawn and gravel paths, half listening to conversation about oil prices and barrels and cricket scores.

'Have you met the new engineer?'

'The Indian chap?'

'Yes.'

'He's very good.'

'Maybe so, but we'll be overrun if we don't watch out. There's darkies everywhere you look nowadays.'

'Yes, our local shop has been taken over by them. My wife refuses to go in there on her own. She says it's not safe.'

'My wife grew up in India. Didn't you darling?'

She nods.

'Was it horribly dirty and savage? I heard they are very backwards.' A blonde woman, introduced only as Jim's wife without a name of her own, asks, her mouth soft and slack over tiny little teeth like a child's.

'No, it wasn't. It isn't.' Her jaw clenches. 'Actually, Indian culture is ancient and has a nobler history than even England's.' She forces a smile.

'Yes, but you're talking about British India, so you wouldn't know, would you?' Jim, his dark hair parted on the side, leans towards her. 'I imagine you were protected on the cantonment from the more crude aspects of the country.' He raises an eyebrow. 'Or perhaps you were in a Colony? With dances at the Institute, a little kutcha butcha, isn't that the phrase?' He grins, looking her up and down, as if he has the measure of her, thinking no doubt that he has humiliated her, revealed her. Stripped her naked in front of everyone.

'Oh, what's that? How interesting? Is this life in the Raj? Tell all, I'm fascinated.' His wife simpers. 'What was the phrase again?'

'Kutcha butcha,' her husband obliges. 'I'm not sure it has an English translation.'

Ada smiles and glances up at Robert, who is watching them both carefully, his face taut. 'You seem to know India well, Jim.'

The old unbelonging creaks like a trapdoor under her, ready to swing open and drop her into a pit that is neither here nor there. A nowhere for nobodies.

'Yes, I served there.'

'Then you'll know that England is a little... chilly, in comparison, isn't it?' Looking him in the eye.

He smirks. 'Your wife is a marvel, Robert. An *exotic* little marvel. Aren't you lucky?'

TAMARA

She avoids the drive through our hometown. Who can blame her? She doesn't need reminding. She remembers well enough a childhood of roaming around all day, exploring the bomb sites grassed over, finding sticky porn mags in the old prefabs, riding the travellers' horses in chained circles on the commons, old farms divided by new roads, orchards, ash trees on chalk downs, blackberries and swimming in the ice blue reservoir. What is it to remember? Memory, with its grooves and paths, well-worn furrows in the brain, along which an impression – shadow, scent, taste – is dusted down, shaken out by a sharp electrical pulse and ferried to the projector-like lobes, where they can be watched over and over. A gloss, a sheen on each of the reworked clips, they are... what's the word? Restored? Rehabilitated? Perhaps just edited will do, by time and good will in the synaptical archives. It's all dust, potentially anyway. A nothing, so what does it matter if each reminiscence is worn shadow-thin and patched up? Who will test the truth of our memory? We will. Prodding and poking about, digging with dead hands to ferret out a lie or untruth, half-truth, no truth. Bone white hands, dig and dig. Exposure. Exposing what was submerged, bringing it into the scrutiny of the open air. A good clean blast of oxygen and light, that will do the trick, get to the quick of it, the nub. Perhaps it's best to forget. There is nothing to see anyway, best to forget. The future will be shaped by all that came before: no need to re-examine the past, it is plaited into the present, filaments that bind. Truth or not, there is no escape, it's always there, nudging you forward. Best to forget, though you can't because we the body always remember.

She takes the ring road, slips through the tunnel under the river and its murky churn, and out the other side, neatly dodging three whole towns to arrive at the new hospital, built on reclaimed ground with a view of the estuary, the white spindles of the wind turbines and the dull suck of silt and mud.

She whispers to her dog. She tells her things she's not even allowed to think, let alone say, and when there are no words that belong to this thing, no words that can match the thick black sludge in her guts, the dog understands just by looking at her. She leans against the warm body, fur tickling her nostrils. The dog averts its gaze but doesn't move. She closes her eyes, trusts the dog to keep her safe. They are hiding behind the shed, her nanna is pulling up weeds – wet-the-beds, buttercups, sticky-weed, clover – from the grass. They can hear her, puffing and groaning as she bends and tugs.

There is a scrabbling sound and the dog jerks away, leaving her alone, leaning on nothing. She scrapes her knee on the gravel as she struggles to follow. The dog is in the back corner of the garden, where the neighbour's fence meets the back alley. It's poking at something, first with its nose, then a paw; before pulling back in a half play-bow, mouth open, tongue loose as if puzzled. She comes closer, head craned to see.

It is a fox, a dead fox. The colour of a dry scab, it's lying on its back, stiff legs up, eyes fixed open, its tongue lolls. The dog has killed it. The dog sniffs at the fox again, nosing its belly, its face. The fox is dead. It doesn't move, can't move. She cries out, grabs the dog by her collar and tries to pull her away. The dog resists, lunging for the body splayed on the ground. The girl cries harder, sobbing now.

'Stop it! Stop it! Bad girl, bad girl.'

Nanna, distracted from her weeding, huffs up behind them. 'What's all this fuss about?'

'She's killed a fox. Look.'

The woman walks right up to the corpse and looks it over, then back at the dog and the girl.

'Cindy didn't kill it, there's no blood on either of them. See?' She grips the dog by the muzzle and lifts its soft lip, exposing clean, sharp teeth. 'The fox probably just died here, and Cindy found it. C'mon, let's leave it where it is and let grandad get rid of it later.' She pulls the crying child close and grasps the dog's collar. 'I've got some ice-poles in the freezer, that'll cheer you up.'

The fox, seizing its chance, leaps up and claws over the fence. They turn just in time to watch it disappear into the alleyway. Nana laughs and lets go of the dog, who runs to the fence, nose down, tail high. 'Clever foxy, she out-foxed us. It was just playing dead, see?'

The child cries harder still. 'But why? It scared me.'

'So it could escape. It didn't want to scare you, the poor thing was scared of us. Dry your eyes now. Sly old fox giving us the slip!'

The child follows her into the house and the cool shade of the kitchen, but for the rest of the day she keeps her distance from the dog, who has proved that she is not to be trusted, just like everyone else.

CLAIRE

Eight kids now. Eight. The ninth slithered out of her last month. She'd nipped into the cinema for the matinee, a bag of toffees in her handbag, scarf on over her head, though why she hid she don't know, it's not like she ain't earned a bit of rest. The kids in school and god knows she don't treat herself all that often. It was an Elvis flick, beautiful as you like that one. What a voice. The new baby was barely showing, a couple a months in, but still the cramps were filthy terrible. She wadded tissue in her drawers to soak up the mess and got the bus home. Den patted her hand and made her put her feet up for the evening. She listened as he fed the kids and sent them off to bed.

She should be feeling better by now, up on her feet, it was only a miscarriage; but oh she hurts, a deep, dark ache. Just women's troubles they say, her nerves are the problem, not her body, she's as strong as an ox really, it's all in her head. Rest, the doctor says. She don't need telling twice, she just wants to stay in bed and sleep. She would swear blind that sometimes she feels like she's being watched, like if she turned around quick enough she'd catch someone just behind her, keeping track, spying. Someone almost recognisable out the corner of her eye; someone who looked just like her, as if she were being spooked by her own ghost. Of course, she won't swear to it cos she won't tell no one. They'd get the men in white coats to take her away and lock her up, daft mare. Rest, the doctor says. Rest. Pull yourself together, she tells herself, because she knows that's what everyone wants to say to her really. Pull yourself together.

Four little ducks in a row. Vanessa, Gayle, Josie and little Bobby. Kicking their legs, squirming, not sitting still, not doing as they've been told. Sat in a line on the dining chairs in the front room. Saucy little bleeders. You can wait there till your father gets home, you hear me? Her head aches, heavy with thick, messy thoughts. But she's managed all the house work and been to pay the gas bill, there's a ham salad with new potatoes and boiled eggs with a nice bit of salad cream for tea. Summers are always the worst. Kids off school, rowdy, bored. Her routine all up the swanny and no chance to have a rest, have a lie down. No rest for the wicked. She must've done something terrible, the way the man upstairs is punishing her.

She goes upstairs to change her pad – she's still bleeding like a stuck pig – and wash her face. She looks awful, washed out, skinny. She must try harder, but she can't think how. The door goes downstairs, and she can hear Den ask the kids what they've done now. She goes down and all five of them turn to look at her.

'They need a wallop,' she says, 'they've driven me up the wall all day.' She sees the look they all give each other. They take sides against her, them against her, her husband and her kids. They don't care how she feels.

'C'mon kids, let's go outside and give your mum some peace, shall we?'

The kids bounce up and dash out, of course he's the good guy, he's the nice one. Don't have to deal with them all day, the whining and moaning, the fighting and shouting, the want want want. No, he just walks in all carefree and he's the hero of the day.

'Tea won't be long,' she shouts after 'em. He's got 'em playing ball in the back garden. They're shrieking and laughing as he pretends one of them is the ball and throws them in the air. He ain't even taken his boots off or washed his hands.

TAMARA

She follows the receptionist's directions and navigates her way through long, emptying corridors towards her mother. She must find the B lifts in the Dickens Wing. The ICU is on the fourth floor, one floor below the maternity ward. This hospital is brand new, shiny and clean. The old hospital, where she was born, is now a development of luxury homes. But before it was a hospital it had been the workhouse, where the poor, the orphaned, the unmarried mothers, the disabled and elderly earned their keep. Imagine the ghosts lingering there.

She is shown to a small waiting area, furnished differently from the other areas, with a sofa, and a poster of a beach at sunset screwed to the wall. A water cooler gurgles rhythmically in the corner. Two women enter: a doctor, who sits opposite, and a nurse, judging by her outfit, who sits next to Tamara watching her carefully for signs of hysteria or unwieldy grief. She listens to the doctor, the words coiling into her ear incomplete and half heard, all the while nodding and sitting absolutely still. She repeats that she understands and that she has no questions; they hand her a series of forms to read and sign. The words vibrate on the page. She blinks.

'How long will she live if I don't sign?'

'That's hard to say. Days, possibly a week or so, maybe less. She's vulnerable to infection you see.'

'Is she awake?'

'She's unconscious.'

'Will she wake up?'

'No, it's very unlikely.'

'Are you sure?' She imagines her mother suddenly sitting up in bed, grabbing her wrists and spitting in her face. Or worse, crying and apologising and asking for forgiveness and love.

'I'm sure.'

Tamara looks down at the forms in her lap. Runs the tips of her fingers over the print as if she can absorb it.

She is killing her. Killing her. She must've said this out loud as the doctor says, 'No, no, you mustn't think of it like that. It's inevitable, I'm afraid, we just don't want to prolong her suffering.' She is tempted not to sign. To let her suffer. Let her linger and sicken and struggle. Her mother will hate this. Hate the hospital, the nurses, the tender care. She will hate her own weakness, almost as much as she hates her daughter. She could abandon her mother right now, just walk away and leave her alone.

The two women look at each other, raise their eyebrows and almost shake their heads. Unprofessional, but they are only human. 'Can we get you a coffee or tea?'

She shakes her head no. Decides. She is not her mother, the daughter is not the mother. No, she is weak, or kind. Same thing. Are they, though? She turns the idea over and signs the permission form for the withdrawal of care. Let them put her out of her misery.

ADA

No matter how she spends her day, Robert always comes home to what he should. She has never lied to him. There is no need: he has no curiosity about her. His assumptions keep her honest, in word at least.

Her life has been rendered down to a series of objects and their care. She changes white cotton sheets crumpled from sleep, wipes fingerprints from windows, picks up Robert's sock left under the dressing table. Cleans a sticky ring from a teacup off the bedside table. Tidies away the pearlescent plastic case for her Dutch cap, discreet as a powder compact. Puts away her lavender hand cream, embroidered handkerchiefs, lace underwear, stockings, tights. Satin nightgown.

She plumps up cushions and swipes dust from side tables and bookshelves. She doesn't read because when she tries she finds her concentration thins and tapers to a dream. She slices cucumbers for her eyes and wraps her face in cold cream. She polishes the silver, taking extra care with the spoons, and replaces everything in the velvet-lined canteen. She rinses crystal tumblers and scours sediment from the port decanter with tiny ball bearings.

Ayah has died, the letter arriving with black edges. It was a short illness, it tells her, she didn't suffer. She makes pepper water and lamb phall which the children refuse to eat. She makes them potatoes and chicken instead. Over one hundred people have died in a riot in Calcutta. It isn't her business any more. She airs out the house, opening all the windows to expel any lingering memory of home. This is her home. England is no longer remarkable and she barely notices its strangeness. Her mother and sister visit, eat cake and drink tea, pat her children on the head. In the evening she watches television, her feet tucked under her; she allows herself a small drink. When Robert is home they eat dinner together and occasionally make love. He tells her she is quiet and wonders what's wrong and she tells him, truthfully, that nothing is wrong, because she can't find the words to describe how she feels and so what she feels can't exist.

At night she watches the children clammy with sleep, her daughter's long hair draped over the pillow. Her son sucking his thumb. She fills them with dreams, telling them they can achieve anything they want. That if they aim for the ceiling they will stay on the floor, but if they aim for the stars they'll have the moon. She tells them they are special just as they are, better than anyone else. She doesn't mention that when they achieve what they thought they wanted and find it meaningless, they'll feel cheated. Empty.

CLAIRE

She sweeps the crumbs from the Formica table into her hand and shakes them into the sink. Some bugger's used a knife on it without the board and bloody ruined it. Now water'll get under the top into the wood underneath and it'll rot and buckle. Nobody else looks after things, they just take it all for granted and leave it to her to sort out. Her lovely table. She ain't even finished paying for it. She should've known better than to get something nice. The chairs match and everything. Oh well, it's done now.

All the kids are out gallivanting, Den's in the garden turning over his potatoes. She's done her hair for once and put on a bit of lipstick. She's decided to take a bit of pride in herself now she's got time on her hands. The kids are growing up. She's got to pull herself together. She's got her monthlies again, twice in one month: Den jokes she should call 'em her 'fortnightlies'. She should see the doctor, she knows that, but she's almost too scared. Silly moo. She makes Den a tea and takes it out, watches him for a bit, the roll and bulge of his shoulders as he lifts and plunges the fork into the soil and then hefts and twists the soil to release the yellow clumps. He's still handsome, even with his dark hair thinning. He stoops to pick up the potatoes and dump 'em into a bucket and as he stands he sees her and smiles, his face lighting up even after almost twenty years together.

'You're a sight for sore eyes.'

'Thought you'd need a cuppa.'

'Ta babe. Almost finished here. What you all dressed up for?'

'Just felt like making an effort.'

'You look lovely. Shame I'm all muddy, or I'd have my hands all over you.'

'Fancy going out later? Maybe a run down the coast for some fish and chips? We could stop in a pub?'

'Yeah, that'd be nice. I'd like that. I'll get meself washed and changed as soon as I'm done. How about that? We could go down to Margate and ride on the wheel.'

She laughs. 'You old romantic.'

'It's nice to see you smile again. You feeling better?'

'A bit. I was thinking I might go out the fields with Margery and Peg. Make a bit of extra money getting the apples in. It's only for a couple a weeks and it might do me good. Would you mind?'

'Why should I mind? It's a free country, and if it cheers you up I'm all for it.'

'All right then.' She takes his empty mug and goes back in. On the outside she looks as calm as a mirror, but she could swing for him: free country my arse, she thinks, what freedom have women ever had? If it's not your father or husband calling the shots it's the kiddies and their never-ending want want want. Freedom is for men and boys. But what's the use of saying anything? What would it change? When has it ever changed? Makes you think maybe it's the way things are meant to be, this is your lot in life and best to make the most of it. Could be worse, she could be married to a bully, or a gambler, or a ladies' man.

TAMARA

The nurse guides her towards her mother. 'We've moved her into a side room, you'll both be more comfortable there.'

She nods, says thank you. Wonders why she is still here, she's signed the papers, what else is there? She wants to run, to escape. But they have assumed she will want to see her mother and she doesn't know how to refuse. The nurse says, 'It will help to say goodbye. Don't be afraid.' Why do people say it will help? Life has been better without her mother in it, why must she say goodbye now? She follows the nurse through a ward, past the visitors clustered around the patients in their beds. Old women mostly. Machines do the body's work. The hospital stink of bodies and boiled vegetables and yeast.

They reach the door and through the small window she can see the outline of a body in the bed, from the hips to the feet. She isn't ready for this. She hasn't prepared. She stops, her head spinning, her breath caught in her throat. She tries to swallow, to breathe, to move. The nurse opens the door and there she is. Her vibrant, raw, vital mother. A woman who refused poor health, didn't trust it after years of her own mother's malingering; dying, sick. Failing.

Her mother who was up early, the house cleaned, spick and tight before she went to work to clean again. Her mother who would sometimes not eat dinner just so she could eat a whole packet of biscuits, who loved smoking cigarettes and laughing at practical jokes. Her mother who never caught cold, never had headaches. Her mother who said illness is a state of mind, a weakness. Her mother who was never tired, never sick, except of hearing her voice, of her constant whining and want want want.

'Are you OK? I know, it can be a shock.'

'I'm fine.'

'Would you like some time alone before I make her comfortable?'

'Pardon? No, go ahead.'

Will she be more comfortable when she is dying? When she is dead? It seems a strange euphemism for letting her die.

She is six, climbing on her mother's bed, sneaking in between boyfriends to claim her mother's body, her portion of love. There is no room. She stands fixed in place, shaking. Watching. The light is dimmed, golden.

The nurse starts unhooking her mother from machines. Disconnecting her from a system. Analogue again. No machine to log her presence, her rhythms. 'Almost done, my love,' the nurse coos, soft and reassuring.

She is four, stroking her mother's hand, watching her mother sleep, holding her hand while she snores, trying to gently wake her so she can have breakfast.

The woman is on the bed, her eyes flicker, almost open. Almost seeing her. Her body tiny, childlike. They have sliced away the poisoned flesh. She steps closer. Touches her mother's hand. Her skin is soft, cold and thin over the bones. They've cut her long nails into sensible ovals. It helps. As if she has been declawed like a circus tiger. The room smells of cut grass, overwhelmingly sweet; somewhere between life and death.

'Does she know I'm here?' she whispers.

'Yes,' the nurse says. 'Just talk to her, she can still hear you.'

'I don't know what to say.'

'It doesn't matter, just so long as you're here.'

She doesn't tell the nurse, I have nothing to say. That it's too late.

She doesn't tell the nurse that the frail, vulnerable woman dissolving on the bed was a nasty selfish bitch. A wolf, a monster, a devil. She doesn't tell the nurse about her last dad dying suddenly at home in his bed, his body tucked up in sleep even though his heart had shuddered to a stop. She doesn't say 'My mother told me she wished it was me that was dead, that I am too difficult to love.'

Or how she is a disappointment. Boring. Ugly. Clumsy.

She can't remember her mother's voice. Only the words.

The room is crowded with our emptiness. She doesn't say anything but places her hand over her mother's and presses it against the bed. We watch.

ADA

This is the currency they leave her with: her body. It's what men want, all they've ever wanted, and how silly they are about it too. Gasping at her naked skin, almost dumb with lust. It's only a temporary power, but it's intoxicating nevertheless. She is rich in this account and may as well be profligate.

At another cocktail party for another of her husband's colleagues, with another round of wives and gossip and innuendo, she is zipped into a blue silk dress and her bracelets clatter and ring like the glass choories of her childhood. She meets Susan while refilling her glass. 'Well, look at you, all grown up. I thought you'd always be the ingenue.' She smiles and performs her part until she can slip away. Robert has disappeared again, charming everyone, as he must, as his duty, for their future, apparently. A man stares at her; he is short but with a thick head of hair and good hands. When she catches his eye he looks away. She waits, staring back at him, returning the gesture, mimicking the language. He looks back and she smiles and, turning to walk up the hall, she tips her head in invitation. He follows her into the cloakroom. He tries to kiss her, but she presses hard on his shoulders, guiding him away.

'Gosh, aren't you pretty. I suppose everyone tells you that.'

She doesn't know his name. His name isn't necessary.

'Not everyone,' she says, leaning back against a vanity unit, the ceramic lip of the sink pressing into her flesh, a firm counterpoint to the soft slip of his tongue. She winds her fingers into his hair and keeps him in place. 'Is my cunt pretty too?'

'Oh God,' he says, pained, 'I've never heard a woman like you say that word.'

She smiles down at him. 'Well? Do I have a pretty cunt?' The word is plump in her mouth.

He gasps and makes a mess of himself, like a schoolboy.

'Can I see you again?'

'No,' she says, leaving him to straighten himself up.

She finds her husband in a corner of the sitting room with a blonde, his hand where it shouldn't be. He at least has the grace to look bashful.

CLAIRE

It's been a funny old day. Rainy, then sun, then cloud, then sun again, like it can't decide what to do with itself. Something's wrong, she feels it in her waters, the knowing, something she can't put her finger on. Probably just her nerves again, but still, the feeling's there. Always there, eating away at her. The girls are fighting, over a dress or a boy or god only knows, but this time they go so far as to smack each other in the face. They're as bad as the boys, worse even, more vicious. Especially Gayle, looks like butter wouldn't melt but she's trouble. Sly. She hears Josie say, 'Hold me gold, I'm gonna punch her teeth in.'

'Oi! Give over you lot,' she shouts up the stairs. 'Give it a rest.' '

All she wants is peace and quiet. She hears nothing for a moment, but just as she starts back for the living room there's a crash and someone cries out.

'Did you hear me? You'll cop it if you're not careful, I'll clump you both one.'

'But mum, she's bust me lip.'

'Shut up or I'll give you something to cry for.' She stays on the bottom step for a bit, listening, but aside from a grumble and a couple of sobs, nothing. They'd had such a lovely day yesterday, the whole family playing rounders up the fields. All of 'em, the kids and their husbands and wives, the grandkids.

Den pleased as punch, squeezing her shoulder. 'We done all right, ain't we girl?' Flasks of tea, sandwiches, cakes, ham sliced, pineapple rings, onions, hunks of cheese, piccalilli, loaves and bottles of beer. The sun snuffing out slowly, not a bad word between 'em. Nothing lasts though.

She goes into the kitchen and with floured hands rolls suet dough into dumplings, one ear out for more fighting. Den comes in with a face like thunder, just as she floats the last dumpling on top of the beef stew.

'What's up with you?'

He just stands there, looking at her, not even taking his boots off.

'I'm sorry my girl. I'm so sorry.'

'What for? What've you done?' She turns to him, crossing floury hands over her chest.

He swallows, presses his lips together, then moves his jaw and tongue as if the words are too big for his mouth.

'For God's sake, Den, just tell me.'

'It's your Bert. He was in a car accident. He's gone, girl, he's gone. I'm so sorry.'

'No. no. Not Bert. That's not right.'

'I'm sorry, babe.'

The room tips up and folds in on itself. She feels as if the rest of the world has fallen away and left only her and Den alive in her kitchen. She blinks. She knew something was wrong. She knew it.

'When?'

'Yesterday.'

'Yesterday? No, no. It was a nice day yesterday. I got all the washing dry, I planted out that new seed bed.'

'Babe, you should sit down.'

On the stove, the stew bubbles up, unsettling the heavy lid, brown liquid spewing down the side of the pot.

'Your tea will spoil.' She turns the gas down and the food quiets, resettles.

'Please sit down, Claire.'

'Who told you?'

'Your Annie. She was waiting for me outside work.'

'Why didn't she tell me herself?' She lights a fag, her hand steady.

'She said she didn't think you'd want to see her, but she knew how close you and Bert were. She didn't want you to hear about it from someone else.'

'Bloody coward. Should've told me herself. She should've come here and faced me.'

'She tried to do the right thing.'

'Whose side are you on, tell me that? She ain't done the right thing in years.'

He puts his arms around her and pulls her in tight. She gives in and sobs.

Lizzy had put her foot down. She'd said, 'He's my husband and she's his sister, so she's welcome.' But they are standing at the back of the church, while the rest of 'em – her mum and dad, Annie and her lot, June, Maryann all grown up, she barely recognised 'em and the others not at all and the two youngest she'd never even met – are up the front with Lizzy. Poor Lizzy, her two little 'uns holding on to her skirt. Both the spitting image of Bert with his gangly legs and black curly hair; his way of scrunching up his nose when he was laughing or crying. She watches her mother. No matter what, she's still her mother and to lose two sons don't bear thinking about. She looks old, her hair greying, her shoulders humped over. Claire's heart bleeds for her, but she's made her choice. The stained glass colours the light as it falls on the polished coffin. The church is packed, which ain't surprising: he was a smashing fella, her Bert. Who wouldn't love him? They don't need the priest to tell 'em how special he was.

She borrowed off the Provident woman and finally got the new hat. Funny how things go. She got the kids new clothes, too. Not all in black: she got the girls dresses in dark burgundy and the boys black trousers and grey shirts. They'll need to get more wear out of it all than a funeral, but there was no bloody way on God's earth she was going to turn up and have them look down at 'em all. They are doing Bert proud. Filling the row, her Den in a black tie and new shirt, the kids well-behaved for once, even singing the hymns. They are doing her proud.

The priest walks down the aisle and behind him the pall bearers carry Bert's coffin. Hard to believe he's in there, her little brother. He was too good, better than all of 'em. Behind the coffin with the kids is Lizzy, who gives her a teary little smile and a squeeze of the hand as she passes. Then the family, who don't even look at her, not even Annie. They walk past as if she was a stranger, nothing to 'em. Her beautiful kids too. Hate gathers in her guts and spreads through her blood into her bones. It wipes out any pain. She starts after 'em but Den holds her back, his hand around her arm.

'Let's go,' he says. 'Before there's trouble.'

TAMARA

Holding hands they dig their toes into the pebbles and climb up the bank. The shingle shifts, tips and rolls under them, inching them back as they struggle forward. At the top they turn to see the others in miniature, still sat behind the stripy windbreak in their deck chairs drinking tea. The sea has been dragged out, as if trapped by its own tide. Today has been a brilliant day. Ice cream, Mummy is there, songs in the car, legs sticky on the hot back seat. Sandwiches and flask of tea, bottle of squash already made up. Bikini for Mummy, swimsuit for her. Nan and Grandad.

Still holding hands they walk towards a huge bowl that's standing up on its side. It's not shiny, but it's a mirror, the mother says. A mirror to capture sound. Like a net for fish. Her mother lifts her onto her shoulders and tells her to listen. What can she hear? 'Everything,' she says.

'Yes,' says her mother, 'a whole world of noises comes across the sea and is caught by the sound mirror. Can you hear them speaking in French? In Punjabi? In Italian?' They giggle. 'Can you hear elephants rumbling, mice squeaking?' Her mother puts her down, sends her twenty, thirty, two steps more away. Whisper a secret and we'll see what I can hear.'

She does. Her mother gasps and her mouth pretends a shocked O. Running to her, she picks her up and swings her around. The marram grass slices at ankles. Her mother's fingers press hard against her ribs, almost tickling. The sound mirror reflects Nanna calling for them to come back. They hide, crouch in the grass, fingers over grinning lips. A seagull with stiff yellow legs watches them, its head cocked to one side. Nanna huffs over the hill.

'There you are. Come on, we're going for fish and chips.'

She runs to her nanna, takes her hand, leaves her mother behind.

'We found a mirror, Nanna, it keeps secrets.'

'So you did. Bloody useless, ugly things. Bout time they pulled those down.'

CLAIRE

She's let herself go. All right, fair enough, but she's past forty now, so it's going to happen ain't it? Middle age spread. Fat tummy, her thighs rubbing together. Saggy boobs, wobbly arms. Skin the texture of lino. It's nice to have a bit of meat on her bones. It was bound to happen, especially after the cancer scare and her op. Does she feel less of a woman now they've cut out all that nonsense? No, she bloody don't; it was a blessing in disguise, putting a stop to all the kids and now she won't have to go through the change and so bloody nice to enjoy a kiss and cuddle and not worry every month.

It's the kids that upset her. Ungrateful, no time for her now, too busy for her. All grown up but still *want want want*. Some days she just lies in bed reading. She's bored. Angry. As tired as she was when they was little but now she's just lost, useless. They make her feel old and over the hill and what's the point? What's the use?

What makes it worse is her girls are off out to work, earning, paying their keep, buying clothes, gallivanting about. Rubbing her nose in it. Going off to dances and the pub, wearing short skirts and little tops, showing off their legs and belly. Bell bottom trousers. What do they look like? Ridiculous. Asking for trouble. Beautiful. Young and slim and bright. Boy mad. Boy crazy. She's told 'em, 'They only want one thing, these boys, and then they drop you. They ruin your life.' The girls don't listen, they think she's never been young. Never been in love. Never got carried away. She says, 'Be good, and if you can't be good be careful, and if you can't be careful buy a pram.' She's trying to make a joke but they don't laugh.

She'd have liked the chance to have nice clothes and go out dancing. To have a proper job and her own money. To be young.

Too late now. Too bloody late. It's eating her up, making her bad, they call it the green-eyed monster and it is a monster, swallowing her whole, taking her over. And sometimes the hurt gets so big she has to give it to someone else, she can't hold it in any more and she says, 'You sure you've got the legs for that skirt?' 'Might want a bigger size.' Or 'If I had your figure I'd wear a nun's habit and be done with it.' Or she says, 'Giving the tarts a run for their money, are we?' But then the nasty spite settles and she feels so rotten, the hurt spreading on their faces and she can't believe what she's done, but too late now, so she says, 'I speak as I find. Truth hurt, does it? If you don't like it, you know where to go.'

Den shakes his head at her but says nothing. Later she hears him talking to the kids: 'Be nice to your mother, try harder, she can't help it.' She feels sick.

When her mother dies she says a prayer for her soul and keeps on with scrubbing the floor, because it won't clean itself, will it? And tears never did anyone any good.

Her mouth hurts, teeth all pulled out, rotten all the way round.

The new dentures rub and hurt. Another wedding. She tries not to cause trouble, holds it in, takes another drink. She fusses over the sandwiches and fancy quiches, shifts the doily under the devilled eggs and straightens the pile of serviettes. She'll tear a strip off the landlady later, the amount she's charging 'em for this. A cold buffet and a room upstairs from the bar. Toilets still stink though, and the brasses ain't been polished in forever by the looks of things. Embarrassing it is. These people will take a mile if you give 'em an inch. Tries to be polite to the new in-laws, tries to remember what her Den said, that they don't look down on her, don't think they're better, they don't even know her, it's all in her head. But she can't help her nerves playing her up. She feels her wilds settling in, but she keeps quiet. Her kids are growing up, that's the third married, she smiles for the camera; only four left at home, three girls and her Bobby, the baby. She holds 'em tighter, loves them harder, keeps 'em close, waits for 'em to get home, wallops 'em when they sneak in late, and always Gayle, the pretty one, heartbreaker people say, troublemaker more like... She holds them tighter and still they get away. Well, let 'em, ungrateful buggers. She tells 'em too, I speak as I find. Bloody kids, who'd have 'em? But she can't tell them the hurts, how she hurts and suffers with her nerves. Truth hurts, that's what it is. The truth hurts.

'Not now, Mum', one of them says. They're running out of patience, sick to the back teeth with her and her taking bad.

Even the doctor says she only does it for attention, and she thinks what? What am I doing? She just wants it all to stop and hold them to her and for them to love her, only her. She's their bloody mother ain't she? It's how it should be, not this pulling away and making new lives for themselves.

And what do the doctors know? The kids finding her and rushing her in the ambulance and how lovely it feels all that care and love and their eyes brimming up, spilling over and so scared to lose her, and they love her, she can see it, and then the stupid doctor says it was a cry for attention, that she didn't take enough to do herself in and she thinks what am I a chemist? How would I know the right amount? But the kids harden and are angry and they go home in a taxi and don't even call Den at work, and they throw away her tablets and stay with her but it's not the same. She feels the rising of her wilds and she clamps her mouth shut to keep it in.

'What now?' her daughter says, all lovely in her wedding dress, lace and frills; not like she had, hurried in a navy utility suit, only her Bert and a pal of Den's there to witness.

'What d'you mean?' she says, and her daughter replies, 'You've got a face like a slapped arse.'

'I'm fine,' she says and smiles again, but it's too late cos the rest of 'em are looking at her like she's done something wrong and she ain't, she ain't, and Den takes her arm and, gentle even though, says 'Let's go home babe, shall we?' And she knows then as she goes that she's saying good bye too loud and too hard and even then can't stop. And outside she hits him, her Den, her handsome boy, she pummels him, belts him, the flat of her fists against his shoulders and he lets her, saying, 'Come on girl, come on girl, that's enough now,' and it's only when the new in-laws, her daughter's new family, come out that she can stop.

ADA

She has rules and keeps to them. The rules keep everyone safe and leave no room for error or mistakes. She will always drive herself to her meetings, far enough away from home, while the children are in school. Each one has his own day, once a week only. Sometimes less. She finds that a lack of familiarity keeps it interesting, and she can't risk anything so foolish as attachment or love to develop; therefore it's essential that banal little intimacies and rituals are avoided. No small talk, no lunching together and never meeting in the evening with its false promise of potential. It's even better if they're married, too, as they understand the rules and are less likely to be silly and imagine a false future. No matter how pleasing a man is to her, no arrangement can last longer than a few months.

They are never from her social circle, barring the odd indiscretion. She meets them out shopping, browsing in bookshops and sitting in cafes, having her car serviced, standing in line at the chemist. It's surprisingly easy if all you want is physical. It must be satisfying, and interesting. She isn't fussed about looks as long as they are clean and healthy. She leaves and never sees them again if they make any demands on her time or are curious about her life. Her play must never encroach on her real life.

She lets them write to her, poste restante, and if she writes back she keeps a carbon copy of her response. She likes to lie in the bath and re-read them, experiencing them over and over. Writing herself into being. Seeing her different selves reflected back in the way these men write her. She keeps them locked up in a box in her wardrobe. They are her collection of lives she could live, is living, almost. She is fascinated by how different sex is with each one in its absolute sameness. Its repertoire of body parts and positions is limited and yet seems infinitely unique. How each one uses his tongue, his hands, his weight; how he sounds. She loves the male body, its strengths and fragility; she loves men and their restless energy, their vulnerable depletion. Stronger, harder than her, different.

She loves the ritual of getting dressed, putting on a costume, playing at being other versions of herself. She bathes and oils her skin, chooses underwear in cotton or silk, lace and nylon. She loves choosing the clothes she will wear and imagining how she will remove them. She pays close attention to how her body feels in the fabric gathered around the nape of her neck, her waist, wrists and knees. She understands that clothes reveal more than they disguise; that the naked body is so uniform in its peculiar animal impulses, its vulnerability and germy aging, and that so few people are at ease in their nakedness, too defensive and ashamed to be themselves.

They occasionally disappoint. One asked why she wouldn't leave her husband for him, that because she was a mother it wasn't right that she only wanted sex. He insisted she must need his love, otherwise she was nothing more than a tart. She laughed and told him she was having her tart and eating it too, he raised his hand to slap her but lost his nerve. She visited another at his house: he was younger than her, and single, but the house had a despairing look about it. Paint peeled from the window frames, tufts of rough grass grew in the cracks in the garden path. The furniture was old and tired; cobwebs furred with dust waved in slow fronds from the ceiling. He led her upstairs but she wanted to leave. She felt sordid, sullied by such a tawdry, ugly place that made no allowance for her fantasy. 'How you brighten the old place up,' he said. At least when he opened the bedroom window the air smelt sweet.

She easily replaced them with others. Others who pleased her, some more than others, like the one who acted as if he was the woman. He put on a show for her, following her directions:

he was the object, she was in charge, watching, she was the one who had to be pleasured. He wore her lipstick and underwear, the lace tight over his cock. She enjoys looking at men, watching them on the street, as they work and sit and move, sees them as they see her and other women, as constituent parts. She feels as if she's evening the score. Delights in watching their muscles roll and contract under their shirts. The curve of buttocks. The taut lines of thighs. The triangle of shoulders tapering to the waist. Hair short on the neck, around the ears. She imagines her mouth, her fingers touching them, holding them. Provoking them. And wanting them, she desires something of herself even more.

Only once she was afraid that Robert was suspicious. He had been watching her closely all weekend, commenting on how happy she seemed, how she seemed like her old self. 'Are you an imposter?' he asked. Later, she found him sitting on the edge of their bed and flipping through the pages of her diary. 'Are you leading a double life? What do you have to hide with your private little code? You know, one day I'll crack it and read this thing.' She froze, ready to lie, but he laughed, just teasing, and gave it back to her, the pages smudged by his invisible fingerprints.

TAMARA

They make up a bed for her. Her mother is strong they say, holding on. It's taking a long time. She is expected to keep a vigil. To watch over the mother, just as a mother watches over her new-born child. Testing the body for breath, for discomfort, for want. She turns away. Scrolls through her phone, scrutinising other people's happiness and ease, then feels guilty and puts it away. Looks out the window at the moon, grey behind a cloud. Listens to the tidal swoosh of traffic ebbing and rising. Voices from the car park; the huddle of smokers under a Perspex shelter. Sounds are more brittle, harsher in winter with no foliage to absorb and soften. In bed the woman moves, shifts her legs. It's just reflexes they say. She checks her mother isn't too cold, rearranges the covers. Dampens the woman's lips with a cotton swab. They've removed her bridge, the frame of her four front teeth. She hates to be seen without it, her mouth half collapsed. Tamara doesn't know how her mother lost her teeth, the story changed and switched depending on the audience and how drunk she was, from being rotten and removed by a dentist, broken in a teenage fall or punched out. We knew, one of us, but that kind of detail is lost in the mass of others.

Tamara isn't a monster: she does the right thing, not one to invite criticism. The nurse comes in, smiles approval at her diligence. They are a perfect tableau of loving mother and child. A daughter accompanying her mother out of life, just as the mother ushered her in. The nurse checks the level in a bag at the side of the bed, looks at the notes hanging over the foot-rail.

'Her kidneys have shut down. It won't be long now. Do you need anything? Can I call anyone?'

Tamara shakes her head.

Her mother's breath huffs and puffs, but it can't blow her house down. Not any more. It catches, pauses, then restarts. Fluid in her lungs and throat bubbles. Her mother doesn't moan, there's no pain as far as she can tell. All that's left of her mother is a body.

She can't cry. Won't give her mother the satisfaction. Her hands shake and she feels as if she is floating, her head separated from her body. She knows this is her last chance to ask her mother why she couldn't love her. Her last chance to say she forgives her. That she doesn't hate her any more. Her last chance to do the right thing, what's expected. That's always been her trouble. Trying to please everyone. Pleasing no one. She says nothing. Not even that she hates her, that her mother was wrong, that she is a spiteful, nasty woman. All the things she should've said, all the things clogged and matted and tangled. It's too late. Doesn't let her mother off the hook. She feels sick.

She has never been allowed to be sick. The bare minimum of care before being told to get up and get on. Enough of this. Her mother's fury when she needed stitches for a cut hand. The scar on her buttock, her grandmother's muttering about neglect and mistreatment. Ignoring the welts and tears, the fear that unpicked the fabric of a little girl. Enough. It has to end.

She steps outside to wash her face, run her wrists under the cold water, the blue veins contracting under her skin. Skin slightly darker than her mother's, but not much. She is more like her than she wants to admit. Like us. We collect and gather and peer back at ourselves. Mirrors line the opposite walls above the rows of sinks. They reflect back at themselves, images rebounding endlessly back and forth until they fragment. Dries her hands on paper towels, that particular smell like damp August hay. It's mid-morning and she almost collides with the tea trolley.

Back in her mother's room the nurse has tidied her up. Tucked in the sheets, combed her hair, plumped the pillow and set her head straight, her arms above the covers, hands folded over her stomach. She looks peaceful, her face slack, less pinched in death. Softer. Tidied away. Neat. Her mother has made all the necessary arrangements. If you want something done right, do it yourself. We all become our mothers eventually. Silenced, poisoned with rage. Mad with fury. But more than that, so much more. All that we've swallowed, remade, taken in our stride. So much more than that.

She picks up her bag and gets ready to leave.

'You're going already?'

'Yes,' she tells the nurse, 'I have a long drive. Do you need me to do anything else?'

'No, no it's just...'

She knows they are watching her as she leaves, shaking their heads at her. Their kindness and cups of tea not necessary. They don't know what to make of her.

It will be perfect if it has snowed, the layer of white reflecting the sun. But it hasn't. There's no magical sign from the universe. No portent, no natural phenomenon that she can misread. She gets in the car. She is not sure who she is anymore. Who is she without her mother? Malleable. Her personality traits pushed and pulled, what's approved of, what's disappointing, less, more. Plasticine baby her mother primped and crimped and cut into shape. The void of freedom, of not belonging, flaps dusty about her head.

CLAIRE

'Look at the state of that, bloody poof! Turn this muck off.'

'Dad! It's Marc Bolan. He's not a poof, he's beautiful.'

'I don't know, bloody boys in make-up and long hair. It's disgusting.' He winks at Claire, making a show of teasing.

'Oh leave 'em be, Den. It's only Top of Pops, it won't hurt 'em. It's fashion, it's all the rage now.'

Claire finishes peeling an orange, splits it in half and passes it to Josie and Gayle on the sofa. She splits her half in half again and hands it to Den, in his armchair next to her.

'Thanks, Mum. See Dad, Mum's with it.'

They all laugh, and it does her good to hear it. Bobby'll be in from his cadets in a bit, wanting his tea and a bath. The other kids are settled, married, got kids of their own. She's a nanna, hark at that! A nanna! She looks around the room, just decorated in a lovely cream colour and a new three piece suite an' all in bronze velour. Bought outright, just like that. Not on tick, not off the Provident or a catalogue: Den just took out his wallet and counted out the notes. The fella in the shop didn't even blink, just booked the delivery and gave 'em the papers. They're even going on holiday in July to bloody Spain! Viva Espana! They've got their passports sorted out, a nice little savings pot for spending money, new suitcases, the lot. Sometimes it feels like she's back to her old self.

She sucks the juice from a slice of her orange. They grow oranges in Spain, though they probably taste even better there, sweeter, fresher. Imagine picking an orange straight from the tree.

She's brought back down to earth by the girls sniding and whispering at each other, as if she doesn't know what they're up

164

to if they keep quiet. Can't give 'em ten minutes before a row starts and here they are almost women.

'Oh girls, don't start.'

Den looks up from the telly. Star Trek is on and, though he hates to admit it, he quite enjoys it. 'Girls, listen to your mother.'

'Tell her.'

'No, stop it, Josie.'

'Mum, Dad, Gayle has something to tell you.'

'No, I don't.'

'Yes, you do.' Josie stands up, her knees pink from lying out in the sun all afternoon. 'If you don't tell 'em I will.'

'Tell me what?'

The girls are staring at each other, Gayle still on the settee, like a girl version of Den, all dark lashes and big blue eyes. She starts to cry and drops her face into her hands like she's in a film. She always was one for drama, that one. Always needing special treatment. Den squeezes Claire's hand and she turns to him, he looks tired suddenly, the colour gone from his face. History repeats itself and ain't that the truth, but then this sort of trouble is as old as time, hardly anything new. Though she thought she'd warned 'em. She nods and turns back to the girls.

'How far along are you?'

'What?'

'You're in trouble ain't you? That's what this is? So how far along?' She puts her last bit of orange on the coffee table and takes a fag from her packet. Den hands her his lighter, his hand shaking.

'Four months, I think.' She doesn't look up, her head still in her hands. Crying.

'No point crying now, is there. Have you seen the doctor?'

'No.'

'So you aren't sure?'

'No.' More sobs.

'Why weren't you on the pill?'

'I was.'

'Fat lot of good that was, then.' She drags on her fag, sighs out a ripple of smoke.

'Who's the father?' Den says. He looks like he might cry an' all. Gayle always was his favourite. 'Have you told him?'

'Yes.'

'And?'

'And what?'

'And what did he say? Is he standing by you?'

Gayle starts sobbing even harder.

'His name is Reuben, and he told her he didn't want nothing to do with it. He doesn't even believe it's his.' Josie folds her arms over her chest, and dumps herself back down on the settee; she always was a tell-tale tit.

'He what?'

'Den, don't get upset. It won't help her, will it?' She turns to Gayle. 'What do you want to do?'

'I want to keep it.'

'Right then. We best get you to the doctors and checked, then I'll see this Reuben's mother and sort this out.'

'I'm sorry, Mum, I'm really sorry.'

'These things happen. We'll get through it.'

'Are you going to kick me out?'

'Don't be bloody daft.'

'Thanks mum.'

'Don't thank me yet, my girl. You'll have to pay your keep, and don't be expecting us to babysit. It's not gonna be easy, but I won't see you out on your own. Under my roof, it's my rules. Understand?'

'Yes.' She wipes her nose on her shirt like a child.

'Now Josie, upstairs please.'

'But Mum...'

'I said out, now. This is between us and your sister and I think you've had your fill of other people's business, don't you? Gayle, we have to speak to this boy and his parents.'

ADA

She has broken her own rules. They are made to be broken after all. She is perched on the kitchen counter, her skirt hitched around her waist, her knickers pushed to the side. The clock ticks steadily above them, keeping a reliable rhythm. Her lover is more erratic. He pushes deeper into her, his hands gripping the flesh of her buttocks as she tightens her legs around him. Her arms around his neck, his mouth close to her ear, his breathing shallow and throaty. A tension spreads from her toes up through her body, a gathering energy of sensation that loosens her from herself for a moment.

The key turns in the front door and Robert calls out, 'Ada?' Her lover tries to pull away, panicked, but she holds on, pulling him in deeper. She knows the routine, and like clockwork her husband thumps up the stairs, his footsteps rising above them. She finishes, almost crying out, muffling her voice in her lover's collar, her cheek soft against the splinters of hair growing on his chin. The toilet flushes upstairs and Robert thumps back down. She flicks on the kettle and turns down the oven. Everything is as it should be, except for the exhilarating rush of her heartbeat.

'There you are, darling.' Robert kisses her on the cheek. 'Hello Freddie, I thought that was your motor outside.' The men shake hands, and Robert grips his brother's shoulder. 'You staying for dinner?'

The kettle boils and clicks off. Ada collects cups and saucers from the cabinet.

'I don't want to be any trouble. I just dropped by to say hello.' He looks nervous, flushed pink, beads of perspiration cluster above his top lip; Ada wills him to calm down.

'It's no trouble, we'll be glad of the company. He should stay, shouldn't he, Ada?'

'Of course he should.' She turns and smiles. 'You absolutely should.'

'There you see, the lady of the house has spoken. You're staying. Don't bother with tea, I'll fix us a proper drink. Brandy? Usual for you, darling?'

Robert clatters ice into one of the glasses, adds ginger ale to the brandy and passes the glass to her. He hands the other glass to his brother. 'Shall we go into the sitting room while we wait for dinner? Leave Ada to get on.'

'Doesn't seem very fair to leave Ada alone slaving over a hot stove for us.' Freddie pulls out a chair at the kitchen table and sits opposite the Waterford crystal vase he bought them as a wedding gift, which is filled with the yellow roses he had given Ada this afternoon. He pushes a blue glazed plate filled with oranges towards the vase so he can rest his arms on the table.

'You don't mind, do you? I think us men bore her.'

'Really? I don't feel bored, in fact Freddie and I were having a lovely time until you interrupted us.'

'Oh, sorry! Shall I go out again? Do you hear that? I'm not wanted in my own home.'

'Don't be an arse.'

The children clatter in through the back door, tousled and filthy.

'Daddy!' They throw themselves at their father and he picks them both up, one in each arm, growling like a bear. 'Uncle Freddie! Save us.' They squirm and wriggle, giggling in their father's arms until he puts them down. 'Supper's nearly ready, go and wash.' They trot off immediately for him, with none of the usual moaning and whining Ada has to endure; they leave a trail of dried grass and seed heads in their wake. She tips a bag of shelled peas into a pan and fills it with water from the kettle, clangs it on the stove and lights the ring.

'Shall we eat at the kitchen table? No need to be formal, is there?'

'Not at all.' Robert sits in his usual seat, his new belly straining against his shirt buttons. His hands cradle his glass.

She lays the table. Freddie gets up to help, his fingertips brushing hers as he takes the cutlery from her. The children return and clamber into their chairs. She watches the peas writhe in the pan, trying to remember what she learnt in school about kinetic energy and heated particles but it's no use, all she can think about is how chaotic a logical process appears, like waves at the shore or the wind. The water froths and threatens to boil over; she empties the pan into a colander over the sink, feeling the steam on her wrists and hands. She tips the half-drained peas into a serving dish and puts them and a shepherd's pie from the oven on the table with serving spoons. Her skirt is slightly twisted at the waist. Robert serves them, one at a time, taking each plate and carefully apportioning the meal according to his calculations. All the while making stupid noises about how delicious it all smells, how wonderful she is. She sits, pressing her thighs together, still feeling the echo of Freddie inside her.

They all eat. Her six-year-old son chews with his mouth open, adenoidal gulps of air and food, disgusting her, for which she is ashamed of herself and so she avoids looking at him and then, overcome with guilt, promises the children ice cream. The two men talk, or rather, Robert talks and Freddie listens, glancing at her occasionally, his brow furrowed, serious. She's had him on this table, on the sofa, in her bed. She thinks about having the two of them together, being held and smothered by them.

'Darling? You're miles away. The children want to get down.'

'Yes, sorry. Of course, you can play in the garden.'

The children charge out, all energy and wild force, sound and motion, rasping chairs against the floor, banging the door shut behind them. She begins clearing the plates, piling them one on top of the other, tipping uneaten scraps into the serving dish.

'Penny for them,' Freddie says.

Robert refills their glasses. 'She won't tell you,' he says, sitting back down. 'Like all women, she is mysterious, impossible to know.' He reaches out as she passes and grabs her about the waist, his face level with her breasts, the knives and forks rattling on the plates she carries. 'My wife the inscrutable goddess.'

'I thought we women were just ordinary people, here to do your bidding.' She pulls away from his grip and dumps the plates in the sink.

'Oh no, we men must worship you, it's our duty. Isn't that right, Freddie?' Robert takes an orange from the plate and begins rolling it in small circles against the table to loosen the skin from the segments inside.

'If you say so.' Freddie finishes his drink with a grimace. They are not very alike, for brothers, Freddie being more slender and long-limbed.

'And yet you don't seem much of a devotee, husband dear, certainly not of me, anyway.' She turns away from them and watches the children playing on the swing in the garden, her daughter standing in the middle of the swing's trajectory and then dashing out of reach each time her little brother arcs forward, his feet flexed ready to kick. They are such strange little brutes at times. Her back has begun to ache, a vicious tightening of muscle around her spine.

'Ouch! The puss cat has claws. Watch out, Freddie, when you find yourself a good woman to marry, and you should get on with it by the way, make sure you have decent armour.'

'I think I shall have a lie down. You can manage without me, can't you?'

'Aye Captain.' Robert salutes her, as Freddie half stands.

'I'll say goodnight now. Good to see you, Freddie.' She can feel him watching her as she goes, his eyes claiming her for himself, clutching at her like a greedy child.

Robert says, his voice low but not low enough, 'Good of you to drop in on her and keep her company. I know it's a chore...'

She climbs the stairs, up and away from them all.

TAMARA

She is seven. Her mother has been called into the school for a discussion. Her mother is nervous and has worn lipstick. The child sits outside the office, chewing the inside of her mouth. A skim of blood and spit coats her teeth. She can't remember what trouble she has to be in. When her mother comes out, she is smiling, she walks like she could fly. She tells her she knew she was gifted, brilliant, more intelligent, beautiful, better than all the others. 'I knew it and now they know it. You're going to be someone.'

'Who?' the girl asks.

'You can be anyone you want.' The mother kisses and squeezes her hard, pressing the air from her lungs. 'You can be anything, just be brilliant.'

CLAIRE

Peg said she was a saint, that she heard about other girls getting sent to the mother and baby home, even now, with the baby being sent out for adoption. Some people can't take the shame of it. In 1976! You'd think people would know better. She can hardly talk, though her and Den never let on to the kids about the boys coming before the wedding, all arse about tit, what's the point of that? But she won't be a hypocrite. Bloody mother and baby home, in this day and age, no different from in her day and before that, poor girls getting sent to the workhouse. Some old ladies still won't go into hospital because it used to be the workhouse. Poor buggers.

But she can't hide the fact that she's disappointed. Till then she'd done so well, raised good kids, kept 'em fed, clothed, clean, holidays in the tent and days out, nice Christmases. She's done her best to love 'em. Now this. Trouble. But bloody hell she won't have anyone else say that. No. No one in this family gets sent away. How can a baby be anything other than a blessing? She does wonder how the girl will cope with a baby. She couldn't even look after her dolly, she left it by the fire and its head melted. Looked like one of them poor thalidomide babies. But she'll be there to help, Gayle won't be on her own. They'll manage, they've come through worse.

'Medway 34517. Hello?'

Listen to the voice on that! Lady muck. 'Yes, hello, is that Reuben's mother?'

'Yes, yes it is. To whom am I speaking?'

'I'm Gayle's mum.'

'I see.'

That took the wind out of her sails, the plum out of her voice.

'He's told you then, has he?'

'Told me what? '

'Well I hate to be the bearer of bad news, but he's got my girl pregnant, and we want to know what you're going to do about it.'

'He told me your daughter has made a false accusation and I'm sorry to tell you that you're mistaken. My son wouldn't do that.'

'Oh really? What is he, a monk?'

Dozy cow, don't she know what boys are like? Maybe they ain't the same on the snooty side of town.

'I beg your pardon! I don't know who you are, or what your daughter has told you, but there must be some mistake: Reuben is still in school.'

'You saying my girl's a liar? Cos I'm telling you now I don't take kindly to people calling my kids names.'

'Perhaps she has the identity of the father confused.'

'You what? Are you saying my daughter's easy?'

Snotty-nosed bitch, bloody plum in her mouth and she don't have to see her face to know she's looking down her nose at 'em.

'Not at all, only that I'm quite sure my son is not the culprit in your daughter's sad situation.'

She could wring her bloody neck, cheeky bitch. 'Listen, your son is the father of my daughter's baby and I want to know what you're going to do about it.'

'Do about it? What do you expect us to do about it? He's sixteen years old, he's a boy.'

'And my daughter's seventeen and to my mind, if they're old enough to make a baby they're old enough to take responsibility.'

'Responsibility? You're not implying marriage are you?'

'What else?'

She has the bloody cheek to laugh. 'This is ridiculous, my son is not the father of your daughter's baby and even if he were I wouldn't let him ruin his life by marrying a girl like her. Do you hear me? Am I making myself clear? Your daughter got herself in trouble and she will have to deal with it. I won't have that child, *it*, mentioned in this house, and I thank you to not call here again.'

She's only put the bloody phone down on her! Hoity toity bitch. Who does she think she is? She's no better than her. She turns to Gayle sat on the bottom stair, listening, chewing the ends of her hair. She looks like the little girl that she is. Pale from all the sickness, and dark rings around her eyes. Scared.

'Did you hear all that?'

'Most of it. They don't want to know, do they?'

'No. She won't have her precious son's life ruined, apparently. She was right stuck up.' Claire lights a fag, then stubs it out. 'Listen babe, you sure it's his?' She don't say anything about how her Gayle can tell a tall one if it suits her, no need to add insult to injury, it won't help anyone to call her a liar.

'Of course, I'm sure. I ain't a tart.'

'No one was saying that.'

'What am I gonna do, Mum?'

'Well I'll tell you what you ain't gonna do, you ain't gonna cry, you're gonna pull yourself together because your baby needs you. You've got us, and we ain't going nowhere. All right?'

'What about Dad? I think he hates me.'

'No he don't, he just hoped for more for you, that's all. He'll come round.'

She dreads telling him about the call. There'll be murders, he'll want to go up there and have it out with 'em. Calling the baby *it*, and as good as calling Gayle a trollop. Bloody cheek of it. What sort of people let their son off the hook like that? As if a girl can knock herself up all alone, her Gayle is hardly the Virgin Mary. She crosses herself.

'Right, that's enough upset for you. Upstairs for a rest. Go on.'

She watches Gayle climb the stairs, her thickening body weary and slower. She should be angrier, should be sad even, she knows everyone is worried about her nerves and her taking bad over all this, but she hasn't felt better in years. She always was a fighter, and woe betide anyone who hurts one of hers. She feels her wilds coming up, but in a good way, like it's getting her ready for battle. Girding her loins.

ADA

She wakes in the middle of the night, alone. The bed linen clings to her damp skin. Night sweats, to be expected at her age, or so she is told. She was dreaming that she was floating on a lily pad on a placid green pond, the Bengal sun stippling her skin. It's so rare that she dreams of India now, and if she does it's unrecognisable. A non-existent place that fuses her childhood with her present, a place of threat and unspoken truths wrapped in a sugar coating. She gets up to change the sheets, going out onto the landing to fetch fresh bedding from the airing cupboard. The light is still on, meaning the kids, adults almost, haven't come home yet. She checks their rooms, just in case, but both beds are empty. She doesn't dread them growing up as much as others seem to expect her to, with their hints and winks at impending empty nest syndrome as if she were a common chicken. In fact it is a relief of sorts, though she notices that the expectations of others aren't particular to her, only to her sex in general: she is a woman and therefore must feel this and that. Her mother and sister seem to enjoy adhering to these prescriptions, as if they need a blueprint to navigate the structure of their feelings and lives. Robert is away on business, somewhere in Scandinavia, Norway perhaps. He probably told her where, and when he'll be back, but she's forgotten. She forgets all sorts of things.

These are the things she must endure, that are part of a woman's lot: memory loss, including the words she needs to think, let alone speak; waking in the middle of the night drenched in sweat, if she managed to get to sleep at all; an inexplicable rage and a dark, consuming depression. She has grown fat, seemingly from nothing: she has a fat little belly now and during the summer had to talcum powder her thighs to stop them from rubbing together and blistering. Her skin texture has changed, her chest and neck now more lined and roughened than her face. She's become invisible. Undesirable. Worse still, is that she can't bear to be touched. Not by anyone. She has lost all desire, all joy in sensual pleasures. She has become a stranger to herself. Unrecognisable, not just in the mirror, but in the everyday experience of just being.

She makes up the bed, tucking in the sheets and smoothing the pillow cases, but can't bear to get back in only to lie awake. She goes downstairs, turning on every light as she goes, eradicating the dark and the compulsion to sleep and rest. In the kitchen she pours herself a glass of water, sips from it then tips the rest away. There is something soothing about watching the water slip down the plug hole. She moves into the sitting room and sits staring at the porcelain figurines of romantic young girls in flowing skirts that Robert buys her for Christmas and her birthday, and the photos of her family, arranged in glass cases around the room. She pays close attention to her furnishings: the tucks and folds of the fabric on the sofa, her cushions, the curtains. The life she has very carefully created. She's not sure how long for. Time often slips by like this, with her sitting and watching and waiting. She stands and straightens the curtains, pulling them tight against the outside, and starts dusting. Moving things and flicking at the shining surfaces with a handkerchief she always keeps in her pocket. It never ends. Never.

She has ended things with Freddie. He had begged her to leave Robert. She told him no, of course. 'But you aren't happy,' he said.

'What does that have to do with it? What does that have to do with anything?'

He is still single, claiming he can only love her. He threatened to tell Robert, to tell everyone, to make her his and his alone.

'You won't. You care too much what people think,' she said, and he replied, 'No, I don't, it's you that cares about that. But I do love you too much to hurt you.'

TAMARA

The journey back is quicker, much quicker. She doesn't linger, no need to hold back, meander. No stopping for petrol, or food or coffee. No need to circle west around London, she can use the tunnel back. The danger has subsided. Her foot firm on the pedal, she presses home. Numb. Except for that filament of rage, just under the skin. The woman just dying, quiet. No anger, no apology, no sour last words. Nothing to hate or cry over, no last-minute forgiveness, no deathbed confession. No sudden flare of love. Just a body slowly and methodically unhooking itself from life. De-animating, organ by organ, cell by cell. She's left her body to science. Nothing to bury, no one to mourn anyway, and she worried all her life about having an unkempt grave: nothing sadder, she'd say, than an untidy grave. No one to care. Rather not have one. So she won't.

She drops off the car and grits her teeth through the commiserations and kind words. She doesn't deserve them. She is a liar, a fraud, a killer. She has been killing her mother her whole life. She thought she might feel better, free. She doesn't know what she feels. Only the pavement under her feet, the bag on her shoulder, the cold air gripping her face and neck. She walks the short distance back to her flat.

The body remembers what the conscious mind will not. How do we trace it back? Those microscopic events that birth these consequences, what created this monster, this wretch? Scientists extract long strands of ice from ancient glaciers and they can reconstruct the past from the trapped air molecules, pollen and other impurities. A globule of water in the sea still retains its river qualities, its condition of being snow, of being drunk, assimilated, excreted. It's very simple. This city is still a swamp, a forest, a charred wreck, a sacred site. This is nothing new. You unravel a jumper to reuse the wool, it's still the sheep, still the pile just sheared waiting to be sorted, carded, spun. Knots and binds. You don't need us to tell you that, but we told you so. We are stories in transmission, legacies, testaments. Hate to say we told you so.

CLAIRE

There she is, that's her babe. Blue eyes open, she's the first to see her. All wrapped up in a little plastic cot. Black hair, soft as feathers. She strokes her cheek and the baby turns towards her finger, mouth open. 'She's hungry,' she says to the nurse.

'She'll be fed in the nursery,' the nurse says, her face set like rough concrete. To be fair, she has given the nurses what for, poor little Gayle in labour for days before they took her into surgery. The Sister all sniffy with her training and protocols, 'we do know what we're doing, madam'; all fur coat no knickers that one, she got her told. 'Listen,' she said, 'I've had eight of 'em and I know when there's trouble.' She was right. Baby too big for Gayle to deliver. The nurse wheels the baby away, her shoes squeaking on the shiny tiles.

In the bed, Gayle shifts, sighs. She pats her hand. 'C'mon girl, wake up. You're a mum. You've had a little girl. C'mon.' The girl wakes, slowly, her eyes sticky with sleep. She smacks her lips.

'My mouth's right dry.'

Claire holds a glass to her lips and cradles her head in her hand. 'Just a sip now. That's it.' She sits back down next to her. 'She's beautiful, you clever girl.'

'Is it all over?' She drifts, only half awake.

'Yeah, all done. It's lovely in 'ere, ain't it? All clean and tidy. Wish I'd had you lot in hospital.'

'Where's the baby?'

'Nurse has taken her off for a feed.'

'What's she like?'

'Perfect.'

A nurse appears at the end of the bed. 'Ah, Miss Shepherd, you're awake. Let's do your checks, shall we?'

The nurse moves about the bed, taking pulse, temperature and blood pressure, making notes as she goes.

'When can I see my baby?' Gayle whispers.

'When she's settled we'll bring her to you, but you must rest. Mustn't she, Mother?' She turns to Claire, who nods.

Then she pulls the bedclothes back. 'Just need to check your wound.' The dressing runs almost the length of Gayle's belly, hip to rib. 'Nice and clean,' says the nurse.

Claire gasps, 'I thought they did it the other way, under her knicker line? She's been butchered.'

'Now now, Mrs Shepherd, no need to exaggerate. I'm sure the doctor had a good reason to choose a longitudinal cut.'

'She's just a girl. That's gonna ruin her looks, a scar like that.'

She could swear the nurse smirks, but she turns away and is halfway down the ward before Claire can say anything else.

'Tamara? That's new one on me. Still, a name is a mother's choice, I suppose.'

'Well, I'd hoped she'd call her Katherine or Isabella after my mother, but there we are. As Den says, she's not mine to name.'

Shirley leans over the pram. 'Pretty little thing, though.' She opens her purse and fishes about to find a five pence piece. She presses it into the baby's palm, then hands it to Claire for the baby's savings. 'How's Gayle doing?'

'You know what these young girls are like. She thought it'd be like having a dolly, all dressing up and cuddles, but now the novelty's worn off. She's too tired to get up, apparently.'

'So that's why you've got her. You're too soft on that girl.' She steps closer to Claire to make room for an old boy to hobble past on the path. 'Any change with the father and his family?'

'No, the bleeders. She doesn't exist as far as they're concerned. Nothing to do with them. Look at her, little angel, who wouldn't want her?'

'Heartless, that's what it is. At least she has you and our Den, you'll see her right.'

'You can count on that. Den dotes on her already: she's the apple of his eye.'

'I don't doubt it. Right, I'd better be off, you know how my Charlie likes his tea on time. Cheerio love, nice to see you and the little one.'

'Keep well, babe.'

She pushes the pram, brand new, shiny, bouncy on its sprung suspension. Nothing but the best for this one, her little princess. She gazes down on Tamara, her pursed lips, her perfect round little face, her little fists drawn up under her chin, and feels fit to burst with love. Truth is she loves having the baby, doesn't care that Gayle is already bored and wants to go out with her friends and go back to work. She's encouraged her. The girl could hardly pin a nappy without catching the baby's skin and if you want something done proper, you have to do it yourself. But oh she's a joy, this little one, and she loves her more than her own if she's honest. She gets to do it all again, only this time round she can get it all right. No mistakes.

It doesn't hurt that it makes her feel young again, gives her a reason to get up every day. She hasn't felt so good in ages. She's bought herself some new clothes, fashionable ones too: shorter hemlines, not too short, nice shoes. Josie said she looked like mutton dressed as lamb, sarky bitch, mouthy cow. Why shouldn't she look nice? Spend a bit on herself? Never had the chance when she was young, why not now? Who says she's too old? She's practically a mother all over again and didn't her own mother keep on having babies at her age?

TAMARA

The baby smiles and smiles at the mother, trying to please. To initiate, ingratiate. The mother turns her back, walks away. The baby ignored, the smiles pointless, failures. She stops trying. The baby understands she will have to find a new way to please, to comply, to be safe. She must learn she has been born to give and reflect love. She mustn't give to receive, that is selfish, cheating, lying. Love doesn't belong to her, it is for someone else. She is a doll, made from many parts with one purpose. A patchwork of her mother, mother's mothers, all those women and their needs, hates, demands, desires. She is not herself, she is them, us. It is not that the dead can come back, more that we have never left. She must fill us up with all we never had.

ADA

Ada half-watches the TV and wonders what to wear this evening. There's talk of going out for dinner and maybe a film. Middle age appears to have rekindled Robert's interest in her, at least at the weekend. They've been going out for long drives in the country and stopping for a pub lunch. He even brought her flowers last week. Just now he is at the barbers, sprucing himself up just for her, or so he says. She isn't complaining.

The kids are sprawling on the sofa in the sitting room; her daughter is flicking through a magazine, lingering over bright photos of handsome boys and pretty girls with long hair. Her son is watching the television, tall and sinewy, his face still smooth except for the beginnings of a moustache above his soft lips. Not quite a man, and yet not a boy either. They are both chewing on cheese on toast, grease shiny on their mouths and fingers. Ada considers telling the girl to throw away the second slice – the poor girl is plump enough – but decides against it. At least for now. It's hard to believe these are her children; that she herself is old enough to be the mother of these young people. When did she become a matron? Middle-aged and dowdy. Her life and choices narrowed even further.

Robert pulls onto the drive. She can tell there is something wrong from the moment he climbs out of the car. Her stomach drops and she sits up straighter. He opens the front door and closes it softly. He has never been a man who loses his temper, he doesn't slam doors or threaten violence, but something about the pace and control of his movements, even from where she sits, feels treacherous. He walks into the sitting room, his coat still on.

'Hair looks very smart, Dad.' The girl looks up and smiles.

'What's left of it,' the boy quips. The kids both laugh and look to their father, expecting him to join in. He doesn't, and the laughter falters and stops. She waits, rigid. The air tightens with his mood, constricting movement, even thought. As if invisible snares crisscross the atmosphere ready to trigger his rage. She wonders what he knows. What has happened. He is just standing there, staring at nothing, breathing slowly. It's the girl, Daddy's Girl, unafraid of him because she has nothing to fear, who asks what's wrong.

'Would you go upstairs, please. I need to talk to your mother.'

'What's up? Dad?'

'Now please.' He looks at Ada, blinks and swallows. His anger softening to fear, at least she hopes that's what she sees. The kids shrug and get up to leave. 'Not you.' He grabs the boy's arm and holds him still. 'You sit down.' The boy sits. 'And turn that bloody thing off.'

The girl whines, 'Why can't I stay?'

'Because this has nothing to do with you. Get out now, before I lose my temper.'

Unused to her father snapping at her, she flees, tears in her eyes, looking back at Ada as she goes.

'What's the matter, Rob? You're scaring us.'

He sits, heavily, in his chair, his hands gripping his knees. 'I had a very interesting conversation with the Saturday girl in the barbers.'

'And?' A cold, slippery feeling of relief trickles through her. What harm could a strange girl do to them? What could she possibly know about her or her life?

Robert looks to their son. 'Why don't you tell us about Gayle?'

'Who? I don't know her, Dad.' All the colour has drained from his face and he begins to chew on his bottom lip, a habit from childhood.

'Don't bloody lie to me. You think you're a man now? Act like one. You've known for weeks and you've not had the guts to tell us. I had to find out from a stranger, in my bloody barbers!'

'What? What did you find out? For the love of Christ, what is going on?'

'The girl, this Gayle, is pregnant. At least three months gone.'

'Don't shout, people will hear you. And what does that have to do with us?'

'She says it's his,' he points at the boy. 'This stupid idiot.'

'Nonsense, he's just a child.'

'Well, evidently not, Ada.'

The boy starts to cry, his face in his hands. She gets up to put her arms around him.

'Don't you dare mollycoddle him! He wants to be a man, he has to act like one.'

'But Robert...'

'No, leave him. He's spoilt and thinks the world revolves around him.'

'But he's upset, you're scaring him.'

'So he should be. You should've seen the state of the poor girl. She was terrified, a tiny little thing too, but at least she had the guts to tell the truth.'

'Perhaps it isn't the truth.'

'Oh, come on, Ada. I know you think the sun shines out of his backside, but this is too much.'

'Is the child yours, darling?' She wants to reach out and stroke his hair back from his face.

'I don't know. Maybe.'

'There. It could be anyone's. What sort of a girl is she?'

'What do you mean?'

'Where does she come from? Does she have lots of boyfriends? How do you know her?'

'We met at the club, it was just fun, nothing serious, it was only a couple of times.'

'There, you see?' She shakes her head at Robert. 'Where does she live?'

'I think she lives over near Green Lanes.'

'Green Lanes? That's the council estate.' She tilts her head and raises her eyebrow. 'Robert! She sees him as her meal ticket, obviously. We all know the type of people that live there.'

'Are you mad? She's a kid, a scared kid. Imagine if she was our daughter.'

'I don't need to, because our daughter won't be so easy or silly.'

'Well, he needs to decide what he's going to do. Do you hear me son? You have to take responsibility.'

'No, he doesn't. That girl made a choice. She could've have got the Pill, or an abortion, they're legal now you know. In this day and age there's no excuse and I won't have my son suffer because of her choice.'

'What about the child? You'll let the child suffer? Our grandchild?'

She shudders at the thought of being a grandmother. 'It has nothing to do with us. It's not his. I will not allow my son's life to be ruined by this cheap girl and her brat.'

'My God, Ada. Listen to yourself.' He shakes his head. 'I can't believe this. You're going to let him off the hook and you're going to turn your back on this girl, this baby?'

'Yes, that's it. I won't have that child, *it*, mentioned in this house ever again. I won't have this shame brought here, not after all I've sacrificed. We are not the kind of people that this happens to. I won't have it. I won't make my son live a life he can't stand.'

'He's my son too, and it's time he grew up and became a man.'

'A man like you?' She glares at him.

'What's that supposed to mean?'

'We all make mistakes. All of us. That doesn't mean we have to pay for it for the rest of our lives.'

'Are you mad? This is appalling, Ada. I thought better of you.'

'That may be so, Robert, but this is how it is. I don't want to hear about this incident again.' She turns to the boy. 'Now, you go and wash your face and compose yourself and I'm going to get ready for our night out.' They leave Robert alone, his head in his hands, and she knows that he will come around eventually because it is the easiest thing to do.

TAMARA

To look at her you wouldn't think she's suffering with her nerves, a nervous condition, and we do look at her, through her, with her. We're vigilant. To look at her you'd never think she can't leave the house on a simple errand without running through the steps it will take to, for example, return a dress she bought online by dropping it off at the post office, and then picking up a loaf of bread, and then perhaps taking her light bulbs and batteries to the special recycling bin. All this needs a plan, a list of steps, a route visualised and thought through.

Poor girl. She suffers the old way, melancholic and prone to sadness and with the newer sort: the jangle and fizz of misfiring neurons, nerve receptors, spinal cord, inflammation; and the less obvious, the virus that lives in the root of a nerve, and like a spiteful mollusc crawls up the channel it keeps to erupt on the surface as a crusty, contagious scab.

She won't classify herself as anxious, as nervous, but she is. We watch her. We know and understand. We remember.

CLAIRE

There's always something with this lot, always trouble of one sort or another. But that's girls for you, trouble. What she wouldn't give for a bit of peace. Vanessa's on the settee crying and wailing, a lump on her face like a Whitstable oyster.

'Oh, he hit me,' she says. 'He hit me.' In front of her two kiddies an all.

'Shush,' Claire says, 'you're scaring the babes.' She don't say I bet you asked for it, cos she don't half come it that one, she'd give her a clump every now and then if she were her husband too. But Den won't stand for it, he's got his principles and hitting women he won't abide, no real man touches a woman he says, so he's gone out after him to see how he likes it. She don't like the boy's chances. Her Den always was a scrappy bugger.

'I can't go back to him, Mum, I can't. Can I stay here?'

'Don't be silly, you're married now. It'll blow over and you'll make it up. You'll see.'

'I won't,' she snivels. 'He's a bastard.'

'Well you can't stay here, there's no room.'

'Please, Mum? Just for a bit.'

'Where will you sleep? I've got Gayle and Tamara sharing with Josie, Bobby in the box room, I've got no room.'

'So it's all right for Gayle and her bastard to stay here, running you ragged, but not me an' my kids when we need you? I get it.'

Claire grabs her arm and squeezes it hard. 'Listen here you, don't you ever call that angel that filthy word again. D'you hear me?'

Vanessa tries to pull away but can't. 'Leave off Mum, you're hurting.'

'D'you hear me?'

'Yes, I hear you. Now let me go.'

'I warned you not to marry that nasty sod, didn't I? I told you what his family was like. They're a rough lot, common as muck with barely a job between 'em, but no, you knew best. You made your bed, my girl, and now you have to sleep in it.'

'You can be so hard sometimes, Mum.' She cries even harder and her two little kids curl tighter into her, clutching her damp blouse. 'I only married him to get out of here.'

'If you don't like it, you know where the door is. And I tell you something else for nothing: don't come back.' She gets up. Tamara will be awake any minute, and the poor little darling gets scared if she's not there to pick her up.

She's never been happier. Pulling the little 'un in her shopping trolley, her little face peeking out the top, chatting away. Shelling peas, eating more than they keep for tea, sweet bubbles on the tongue. Sitting on the back step, the warmth of her little body leaning against her, the sun high over them. The leaves are turning. They sing nursery rhymes and she teaches her to read. They play hide and seek when she's making up the beds and cleaning the house, though that takes a back seat to the little one and she doesn't even notice. Sunday mornings in bed with Tamara between them. Den passing them cups of lemon Lift from the Teasmade. The donkey on top of the wardrobe brought all the way back from Spain, with a child-sized sombrero on its head. Her mother's plaster St Francis and the glow-in-the-dark Madonna from Lourdes, the small bottle of holy water next to her brush and comb and lipstick on the dressing table.

They roast chestnuts on a pan over the fire. She stuffs a chicken with onion and some sage, a bit of thyme, rubs a lemon over the skin. The little 'un cries, 'Is this Jenny? I can't eat Jenny.' Tears streaming, crying her heart out she is, for poor Jenny.

'No, it's not Jenny,' she tells her, taking her up the garden to the chicken coop and showing her Jenny pecking about, but she won't be comforted: 'I can't eat my friends.' While the rest of 'em eat, chicken grease on their lips, she makes the babe some pea soup.

You spoil her they say.

But she loves her for her tender heart and gentle ways. She's an offering she could never make herself, and it comes from her, from her flesh and blood, her soul, her heart. She feels folded into the child's imagination, the way she sees the world, as if the universe unrolls itself for her, showing her its secrets and the ways of speaking to its materials, its parts. Tamara is her otherness, a chance at being the girl she might've been. Dancing and charming and singing and skipping over gravity when it suits her and only her. Capturing the wildness and the thrilling and quickening of herself. She hears the fairies, the witches, the animals speak just as clear as the child. How huge, how mysterious life becomes; they hold tight to each other, the little one and her. They whisper to each other, lean in warm and, when not side by side, look close across the room and know.

'You shouldn't spoil her,' they say.

She won't tell them, can't tell them how she gathers up the child in her arms and is soothing her own aches, the hurts, the rage. Another chance, another love. They're just jealous.

TAMARA

There's a thin blade of light across her threshold. Someone is inside. She hears movement. Has her mother followed her here, is she haunting her already? The door pulls open. 'Tam. Oh darling.' Pav holds her arms out, her face tucked in around an expression of concern. She steps forward, letting Pav hold her for a second. 'You OK? Of course you're not. C'mon, let's get you in.'

There are shopping bags piled on the counter. Flowers on the table. Her friend's presence changes the flat, makes it real. It takes a new shape, solidifies. Is lighter somehow, warmer. Something is simmering on the cooker. Pav picks up a velvet cushion, strokes it, plumps it and tucks it into the corner of the sofa. 'Sit. I've made you a lentil casserole. Can you eat?' Takes her coat and hangs it by the door, all the while watching her for cracks and leaks.

'When did you get here?'

'This afternoon. I phoned and left messages and when you didn't reply I thought sod it, I'll use the key and come over. I've bought breakfast and some other bits too. You don't mind?'

'No, I'm happy to see you.'

Pav scoops her hair up and twists it into a pile on her head with a band. She's able, just as her nanna was able and her mother too, on a good day. Making everything seem easy: clean house, clean person, jobs done, functioning. Capable. Simple things that she finds almost impossible. Exhausting. Pav sits on the sofa next to her and puts her arms around her, holding her close. 'Oh, come here.' Obedient, she rests her head on Pav's shoulder, the weave of her shirt pressing against her cheek. She can smell her perfume, the fading floral scent of fabric conditioner.

'I'm so sorry. I can't imagine how you feel. It's so awful.' She feels the convulsions of Pav's body as she begins to weep. Pav holds her tight. Sobs. Tamara pats her hand. Listens to her breath catch in the hollows of her body. The live heat of her exchanging through her clothes, the air, the molecules between them. Pav pulls back and strokes Tamara's dry face with her fingertips before wiping her own damp face. Smearing the tears across her cheeks.

'God, I'm sorry, you're in shock, and here I am crying. I just feel so bad for you. I know you're not a fan of all this, so I'll just say it once, ok? We all love you, you know? We're here for you. OK?'

'OK.' She nods and makes herself look Pav in the eye for a second. 'Thank you.' She squeezes Pav's hand.

'Let's eat. Shall we eat?'

She nods.

'Table or sofa?'

'Sofa.' She tucks her legs under her, curling into the corner.

What are you crying for? Here come the waterworks. Give it a rest or I'll give you something to cry for. It sounds worse than it is, it's a tough world out there, you have to prepare your children. Crying is for sissies. For cowards, For babies. For victims. You can't let the bastards see your weakness. It was for her own good. Their own good.

'Is it OK?'

'It's great, thank you. I haven't had anything since yesterday.' They sit at opposite ends of the sofa. She rests her spoon on the bowl, leaving some. Because she can. She doesn't have to clear her plate now.

'You don't like it?'

'Oh yeah, I love it. I just can't eat it all.'

'Fair enough.' Pav takes the bowls and spoons and puts them in the dishwasher.

CLAIRE

'Let her go,' Den says, 'we knew this would happen. She needs her independence and we need our lives back. We've had our kids, Josie and Bobby have flown the nest, we can start going out and about again. We can have our holidays, I'll even redecorate for you. Come on, look on the bright side, the babe will come and stay still, we'll have the best of both worlds.' He rubs her tears away with a work-toughened thumb.

'But she won't cope, she's never here with her. She hardly knows her. Always off out with one of her fancy men. She don't know the babe's routine, how she likes her breakfast, her bedtime stories. The other day she tried to feed her bacon – what sort of a mother don't know her child? I'll tell you: the sort that don't deserve their baby. When does Tammy ever ask for her? When does she go to her? Never. Gayle won't be able to manage, and I don't think the baby can either. She needs me.'

'My babe, you've done that girl a world of good but maybe we should let her stand on her own two feet. She might do better than we think. Tam is her little girl and she's not a baby any more is she? She starts school in September. It's time. The flat's only round the corner, we can pop over any time. Don't you think it's time you had a bit of peace and quiet for yourself?'

'She only wants her now the hard part is done, now she's potty trained and clean at night, now she can dress herself, now she's chatty and fun. I won't have it, I won't let her take her, I'll go to court.'

'But she's hers, Claire, we have to let them go.'

'Den, my heart's breaking.'

'I know my girl. I know. But it's not the end of the world.'

Her boys are loading Gayle's bits and pieces into their work van. Her own sons are helping to break her heart. Tamara's toys have been boxed up. It turns out Gayle had been planning this for months, buying kitchen bits, saving up for furniture and booking delivery for when she was moved in. Eight floors up in one of them new blocks. Central heating, fitted kitchen, balcony, views all the way to the river. She makes it sound like a palace. Silly girl, let's see how she copes on her own, the washing, the cleaning, the cooking, the listening and chatting and helping and wiping and smiling and singing and cuddles and brushing and feeding and changing and drudge.

She walks outside, arms crossed over her chest, fists tucked under elbows. Stands on the front step, flanked by roses and hollyhocks, fuchsias like Victorian bonnets. Gayle is holding Tamara by the hand, directing her older brothers as they disappear her belongings into the van, emerge empty-handed. They all take sides against her, even her boys, her beloved first-born boys.

'Is that it?'

'Yeah, I think so.'

'Right, let's go then.' Paul shuts the doors and sees her standing there. 'Mum! I was just about to pop in and say hello.'

'Ma! Didn't see you there.' Stephen says, joining his brother striding up the path, everything about them identical, even down to the way they flick their hair from their eyes, the way they squint the sun away. She receives their kisses, one on each cheek. With Stephen's kiss comes a command: 'Don't make a fuss now, Mum, will you?' He's always been bossy, always thinks he knows best. She don't answer.

Gayle stands on the path, halfway to the gate; she looks scared, but she squares her shoulders like a boxer about to come out of their corner. Holding tight to the little 'un's hand, she says, 'We'll be off now, Mum. Come see us tomorrow? I'll get us some fish and chips.' When she don't answer, the girl says, 'See you later then.'

She watches as they go, little Tamara following her mother but looking back at her, confused, her little mouth set in a grim line. She waves, and blows a kiss to the child, who starts crying and struggling, stretching her hand out to her before Gayle tugs her away and they disappear behind the privet and into the van like all the other things Gayle is taking from her.

'Well done, love.' Den puts his arms around her. 'Well done.'

'I'm not a child,' she says. 'I can keep myself together, you know.'

The van's engine fires, drowning out the crying and wailing and calling for her, and they pull away. They've gone.

TAMARA

The second hand of the clock moves even more slowly than on a Sunday. The fridge hums, occasionally shudders. The TV chatters from the front room next door. The tap drips. They've taken Cindy in with them so she can't help her eat; without her she's stuck there. She is eight and can't leave the table until she's cleared the plate. She must eat all the food. The fat, the sinew, the congealed gravy, the mushy vegetables boiled until their molecules break down. She has given up chewing the gristly meat. Just tries to saw it into smaller and smaller pieces she can hide in her pocket. Has managed the potato waffle and the peas. What she doesn't eat tonight she'll have for breakfast tomorrow. It's past bedtime. Her mother has been in, checking her progress. Hurrying her up, telling her to not cause trouble. She doesn't mean to make trouble, she just can't eat it. It makes her sick. She can't swallow. She can't put it in the bin because they check and she isn't allowed to use the toilet till she's finished. She's trapped.

He comes in, new dad. Stands over her and watches. Shakes his head and grabs her fork, spears a chunk of the meat and pinches her nose, shoves the food into her mouth. 'EAT IT.'

She chews, tries to swallow and gags. Spits the food onto the plate. She is crying. He picks up the plate and throws it against the wall; gravy slimes like the ghostly traces from that film she liked. He shouts to her mother, 'This THING causes all the trouble, why can't we get rid of it?'

She is a thing. To her he says, 'I hate you just as much as you hate me.' But at least he doesn't touch her.

CLAIRE

To be fair, Gayle seems to be doing all right. Claire sits on Gayle's new settee, a fag burning away in the heavy brown glass ashtray on the chrome and glass coffee table – all bought on the never-never of course. The place is spotless. A bit bare, but then she has just started out. Winter sunlight drifts in the big windows. Gayle is ironing in the corner, steam gushes and flares from the nozzle, like an effect on Top of the Pops, half hiding her as she presses and smooths the clothes in the pile. She's still got a bit of tan from the summer, always does, this one.

Tamara comes into the room, a book under her arm. Her hair is in perfect plaits behind each ear, her centre parting ruler straight. Gayle's dressed her in green corduroy trousers and a green blouse. Like a little fashion plate, a mini version of herself. She no doubt thinks the kiddie looks sweet, but Tamara hates things tight around her tummy, can't stand clothes that rub or itch or irritate. To prove her point Tamara scratches and pulls at her waistband. She stays by the door, still, only half there, her bottom lip sucked in.

'There you are! I thought you'd got lost.'

Tamara shakes her head.

'Sit with Nanna then and show her your reading. Listen to her, Mum, she's amazing. The teacher can't believe it, says she's reading like an eight-year old, and doing all her sums. Go on, Tam-Tam, show Nanna.'

She sits next to Claire and opens the book. Claire slides her arm around the child and she leans in against her, her little body softening.

She reads, 'Peter, Jane, a dog, a tree, a ball.' Her finger underlining the words as she whispers them.

'Oh, very good,' Claire says.

Gayle looks up through the steam. 'No Babe, not that book, that's a baby book. You can read much better than that, can't you? C'mon now. Don't be lazy, go and get a proper story book and read to Nanna. Like I said.'

Tamara turns her face to Claire. Tears float across her eyes, collect in her lashes and roll over her cheeks. She don't make a sound, not a sob or a sigh, nothing. Claire pulls her in tight, snuggles the girl into her chest. 'It's all right, baby, don't cry.'

'Oh, what's up now? Always the waterworks with her.' Gayle slams the iron down on the board.

The little girl jumps and cuddles in tighter. 'Perhaps she's tired, she's only five, Gayle. Maybe she don't wanna read.' To the kid she says, 'D'you not wanna read now, my baby?'

Tamara shakes her head, a shiny bud of snot under her nose. Claire pulls out the hankie tucked into her sleeve and wipes her face, kisses her forehead.

'No, Mum, she's a spoilt little madam, she's a nightmare. She don't sleep, she's fussy all the time, she won't eat what I cook just pushes her food around the plate for hours, she don't like her clothes I buy her and look at them, they're beautiful, cost the bloody earth. I can't please her. Yesterday I made jam tarts with her, played with her dolls, read with her and she sulked all the way through. I try, Mum, I really do. There's no getting through to her.'

'Just let her be, Gayle. She'll come round.'

'You know she's started wetting the bed? It's getting so bad I had to smack her the other night.'

She wants to say, let her come home with me, where she belongs. She wants to say, stop being so hard on the baby. She wants to say, she's not your circus monkey you can show off. But she don't. Den's warning not to interfere, not to stick her nose in where it's not wanted or risk not seeing Tamara at all, chokes the words off in her throat. She swallows the words down. There's no talking to this one anyway, she's all or nothing, mother of the year or wicked witch. Hot one minute, cold the next.

She strokes Tamara's hair and tilts her face up. 'Listen to me, babe. Are you listening?' The child nods. 'I want you to try and be a good girl, OK? I want you to eat all your dinners and do what Mummy says. I want you to help your mummy and make her smile, can you do that?'

She nods again. Claire squeezes her tight, Gayle watching every move. 'Good girl. Now go and kiss Mummy and then play in your room for a bit. You can come and stay with Nanna and Pops soon, yeah?'

She slides the child off her lap and pushes her gently towards her mother. Her little body stiffens, then gives in and she walks over to Gayle who strokes her head like she's stroking a spiteful cat. At the door she turns and looks back at Claire, her round little face pinched tight, unreadable. Unrecognisable.

ADA

Ada received the call. Someone asking for her son, and if she might tell him that she called. Giving her name and telephone number in a voice estuary-flat, nasal, the consonants dulled. The child, a teenager now, turning up like a bad penny. An undead ghost that has been ever present, haunting them despite Ada's best efforts to exorcise her. The others are excited, wanting to finally meet her and, she suspects, make sentimental amends. She asks Robert, why should they meet the child? What good will it do? We don't know her. She has a family. But he is certain they must welcome her. He confesses that he used to watch the little girl, that he'd park outside her other grandparent's house and wait to see her, to reassure himself she was ok. He watched her playing in the garden. He saw the mother, the girl become a woman. The child seemed happy, well-cared for. The way he says it is as if it exonerates him, this cursory spectatorship. They arrange a visit. The son will meet her first, then introduce her to his wife and his other children. Then, when they are well-acquainted, she will come here, and meet Ada and Robert, their daughter and her family. The others agree that seems like the right thing. She still hasn't told her mother or her sister.

They will be arriving around four, tea-time. She wonders what to wear, how to speak to the child. Robert whistles as he dresses, it's like Christmas morning for him. He is light on his feet, smiling.

'What will we tell people? How will we explain her?'

'What does it matter? We tell them the truth.'

'I don't think this is a good idea.' She pats face powder on to her skin.

'You just don't want to face up to your feelings about her.'
He puts his house shoes on.

'What feelings?'

'Guilt, for starters.'

'I have nothing to feel guilty about.' She snaps her powder compact shut.

'Shame then.'

She turns on her stool to look at him. 'Perhaps I am ashamed. Perhaps I am.'

'We all should be. But what good does that do now?'

He thinks she is talking about the child, only the child. Poor, simple Robert. And just like that, some of the past catches up with them.

CLAIRE

'Mummy's got a new boyfriend.'

She's staying over the weekend, to give Gayle a break. To look at her, you'd think she's fine. Clean, fed, looked after. Something's wrong though. The bright little girl has gone, leaving only her shadow in her place. She picks at the skin around her nails.

'Another one? Don't do that, babe, you'll get a whitlow. C'mon, help me pick the strawberries and we can make jam.'

She's worrying herself so much it's making her bad. She's seen the doctor and he tells her to rest, not to worry. He won't give her any more tablets though, will he? All is well, they say. Den says she's imagining things. That she just wants the baby to come back, so she's telling herself stories to make it happen. He says she shouldn't come between a mother and her child. That she can't interfere. As if she would. Her wilds are up. Her troubles. She feels them bubbling in her blood. Den says Gayle's entitled to her own life. To love. Even Josie, and let's face it there's no love lost between her girls, says Gayle's all right. That she's doing her best. They all say, You idolise that baby, she can't do no wrong in your eyes. They say, maybe the kid is causing trouble. She's been spoilt. What they mean is, it's all her fault. She's too soft on the girl, she's made her like this.

'He's not nice to me,' Tamara says. 'I don't like him.'

'I know you don't, your mum told me.'

Gayle had phoned her, her voice flint hard, ready to spark. 'That kid is impossible. She won't let me be happy. Always causing trouble with Jeff, I mean, he's trying so hard with her, buying her treats, taking us out for the day. She's just so moody.'

'D'you want me to talk to him?'

'No, Mum, don't make trouble. She'll have to learn.'

'She'll come around, it's just new, that's all.'

'You don't know her, Mum. She just won't fit in. She won't try. She's hateful.'

'She's only six! '

'Exactly, old enough to know better. She never leaves her room when he's here, just sits in there, her nose in a book, sulking and when she does come out she's rude. Little miss know-it-all, contradicting everything I say. We took her to the zoo, all that way, all that money. D'you know what she said? I'm bored. Bored!'

'Maybe she was bored.'

'That doesn't matter, Mum. She should be more grateful, rude little shit. Keep her mouth shut. That brat has a lot to answer for. She's the cause of all my problems.'

'Don't say that, Gayle. She's a little girl.'

'That maybe so, Mum, but she's a liar, she makes up stories to cause trouble between us.'

'What sort of stories?'

'Stupid things, disgusting things I know can't be true. She still wets the bed, you know, it's filthy. The other day I ran out of toilet paper and she wiped her shitty fingers on the wall! On my bathroom WALL.'

'She's just a child.'

'Since when was that an excuse? You wouldn't have put up with this from any of us kids. You'd have walloped the living daylights out of us. Anyway, you don't know her. Everything I do for her, all I've given up. I can't have a life of my own as far as she's concerned.'

'That was your choice. Nobody made you have her.'

'Don't I know it. I live with it every day, you don't have to remind me.'

'She can come back here, if you like.'

'To you? The perfect mother? I don't think that'll help, d'you? With your nerves and your troubles. You're not well, Mum. You tell us all, over and over, how ill you are. How much you ache. I hate to say it, but you're as bad as one another. Always needing attention.'

'Don't be nasty, Gayle. Don't hurt me.'

'I speak as I find, that's it, ain't it Mum? If you don't like it you know where to go? Ain't that the family way? Your way? You've told us often enough.'

The girl squats down, her knees pressing her shoulders. She flicks a squashed strawberry into the bowl.

'I wish I had my own daddy, like other kids. My own daddy wouldn't hurt me.'

'Why do you say that? Is someone hurting you?'

The girl stiffens, looks away.

'Tamara? Does he hurt you?'

She nods, watching Claire out the corner of her eye, like she's sizing her up. Claire hates to think it, but the girl looks shifty.

'Tell me the truth now, don't lie to me, you know what happens to little girls who lie?' The girl nods. 'They have their tongues cut out, don't they? So think carefully before you answer. Does he hurt you?'

She looks so small, crouched there in the dirt, her hair straggling loose from her pigtails. She must look like the father's family, it's hard to see her Gayle reflected in the round little face. She looks down at the ground, her chin wobbling, but when she looks up at Claire, there are no tears. Her face is blank. She shakes her head, no. Then stands up, wiping her sticky fingers on her dress. She looks Claire straight in the eye, like a little grown woman, and says, 'But I'm not a liar, Nanna.'

She can't answer the girl. She's so tired all of a sudden, so weak, she just wants to lie down and sleep and never wake up.

TAMARA

'How did it go, was it really bad?'

'Yes and no. I just signed some papers and sat with her till it was over.'

'Was she awake or aware of anything?'

'No, but the nurse said she knew I was there.'

'Well, that's something isn't it? That must help a little.'

'Maybe.'

'I think you did the right thing, I know you didn't get on, but I really think it's important that you were there. I mean she asked for you, that shows how much she loved you really. She's your mum, the most important relationship you'll ever have.'

'I suppose so.' She sips her tea. It's dark outside. Her mother has been dead for eight hours.

'Do you know in all the time we've been friends I've only met your mum once?'

'Really?' She is only pretending to not know this.

'I think so, she wasn't at graduation was she?'

Tamara shakes her head. Her mother was on holiday soaking up the sun when she graduated; she wanted a copy of the photo, though, Tamara in her rented cap and gown, holding the prop scroll. She put it in the cabinet next to her school photos.

'Then the only time I met your mum was at your wedding and I don't think she stayed long.'

'No. She left after the cake was cut.'

'I don't remember speaking to her or even saying hello.'

'That sounds about right. She wouldn't want to give the impression that she was happy to be there.'

'Jesus. Was she always like that?'

'No, not always. She could be fun and loving but then it would change. Like she was two different people; or I was and she was reacting to me. She could be so difficult to please. Angry all the time. But then it couldn't have been easy for her. I was a hard kid, I think. Disappointing. We didn't have a pot to piss in. She was young, didn't want to be tied down. I lived with my grandparents till I was about four, then she got a flat off the council and we moved out.'

'What was that like?'

'Ah you know, pretty shit.' Least said, soonest mended, though there's also a problem shared is a problem halved. Take your pick.

'You never talk about this. You never even told me why you stopped speaking to her.'

'It's a long story. Boring.'

'I doubt it's boring, it's pretty hard-core not speak to your own mother. I can't imagine being without my mum, no matter how annoying she can be.'

'Let's not talk about her anymore.'

'Are you sure? It might help. You shouldn't keep these things bottled up. I know you like to keep your life in its separate boxes but it's not good for you.'

'Honestly, let's leave it.'

'I really think it will help if you open up.'

'Oh for God's sake, Pav, please stop. Please SHUT UP.'

Pav pulls back, sitting deeper into the sofa. She takes a sip from her glass as if she is shielding her face. She looks away. Tamara stands, her throat burning, raw, unused to shouting. Then squeezing shut. Cutting off her voice, her ugly rage that spits and shivers and buzzes in her meat. That's enough of that. Starve it of oxygen, kill it. Smother it.

'I'm sorry, I'm sorry. I'm going to lay down for a bit.'

ADA

Tamara is sitting on the sofa, Ada's newly upholstered sofa, which still pleases her with its fresh, clean fabric and neat tucks, though perhaps it will be less so after having the girl in her grubby clothes sit on it, a teacup awkward in her hand. She wonders why young women these days, particularly clever ones, go out of their way to be unattractive and unkempt. She makes no comment. These visits from the girl are rare and, even though she suspects she only visits to ask for money, Robert is enchanted by the girl; a transmutation of his guilty feelings perhaps. He is sprawling heavily in his armchair, hanging on the girl's every word.

'I can't get over how like you she is!' He beams at Ada. 'Even the way she holds herself!'

Ada smiles. 'Yes, very.' But she can't quite see it herself. Not really.

'How do you like Durham?'

'It's great, I love it. I'm sharing a flat with a really good crowd of people.'

'A crowd? In a flat? That must be a squeeze.'

The girl, Tamara, blushes and hesitates before breathing a little embarrassed laugh. 'Yes, I mean my friends, there's four of us. We just say we're a "crowd". Silly isn't it?'

'No, not at all,' Robert says, flashing Ada a look.

'I just think that for someone studying English Literature, such as yourself, it's of utmost importance to be precise with your language, your expression.'

'Yes.' The girl pronounces the word with care, watching Ada's reaction.

'And do you come home often? Your mother must like seeing you.'

'The last time was Christmas, but I'm only staying a week this time before I go back, I managed to get a job for the summer up there and we get to stay in the flat.' She looks about the room for somewhere to put her cup and saucer. Robert reaches out and takes it from her, placing it on the side table by his chair. Her relief is obvious. Ada watches her closely. Her earnest need to please and connect with them signals something false about the girl, something untrustworthy. Ada really can't see any resemblance between her and the family at all. She is all her mother's side. In character at least.

'How are your studies? I do envy you, and your opportunities. I'd have loved to have been able to read for a degree, wouldn't I, Robert?'

'Yes, you would have *loved* it.' He rolls his eyes at the girl.

Ada ignores him. 'It must be wonderful to read all those classics of literature, so timeless and transcendent. Do you all sit and discuss them in seminars? I'd have liked that very much. We learn so much about human nature from books, don't we?'

'Well, uhm, yes. I suppose we do.'

'You don't sound very sure for someone in her second year of university.'

'It's just we don't think about literature like that anymore.'

'Like what? It's literature, how can the way we think about it change? It isn't fashion, books aren't hemlines.'

The girl closes her eyes for a moment, her lips forming the shapes of words, as if she is rehearsing a speech. 'Our professor tells us we must reject all claims of universality when it comes to the Western Canon of literature. She says that most of the classics are written by DWEMS and limited therefore in who and how and what they represent.'

'DWEMs? What on earth?'

'Dead White European Males. Professor Agnew says their time is up, and we must prioritise questions of polyvalency.'

'Well, that puts us old white men in our place! So this polyvolly...?' Robert chuckles, enjoying himself.

'Polyvalency.'

'That's it, what a word! What does that mean?'

'Well, a hybridity really, looking at many ways of being, not just one ideal. I'm still learning, I'm not an expert.'

'Quite, so if you aren't an expert you should take care not to use your education as a cudgel against others; especially when it's flash-in-the-pan ideas that don't hold up against centuries of tradition.'

The girl deflates and it pleases Ada for a moment. She is jealous of course, of the girl's education, her confidence, her intellect; but worse, she has a sneaking sense that what the girl says is right and, if she is honest, something she has suspected but not had the courage to question or even acknowledge to herself. She clenches her jaw and pulls herself in tight as she feels as if she might fall into nothingness, that a blank space has opened up within her. She hates the nothingness and decides that the feeling belongs to the girl. She hates her and everything she is.

'Would anyone like some cake? It's chocolate, I made it myself.' She rises, taking herself and her hatred to the kitchen, where she bites down hard on her fist.

CLAIRE

She'd cut her nose off to spite her face with her attention seeking. That's what they think. She knows different, she knows she ain't got a choice. The wilds carry her off and away and under. And the tiredness, the ache and pain she has, what else is there but to slide under the surface of herself and wait it out? To climb into the dark silent spaces? Like an animal she wants to crawl off and not come back. How else do you make it all go away?

But they find her and take her to the bright white hospital, and like angry, busy mothers they prod and stare and lift and turn and clean out her guts of the black sludge. Then deliver her to a new doctor, new nurses, who turn down the lights and put her to sleep so they could put the kind electrics to her head and fizz the dark away. It works, better than the tablets and the rest and pulling herself together and getting a talking-to. Her wilds have been burnt up, singed off. Her head rings like lead crystal.

The family stand around the bed, looking at her. 'What's the matter this time?' One of them asks. She knows them, they are her children, her husband, people she loves, has loved till it has killed her, wrung her dry but she can't for the life of her remember their names. Only the strange shapes of their faces, the bony points of their hands. How they look when they cry, laugh, lie; how they sound when they think no one is listening.

She is allowed into the day room. A circle of chairs. Other ladies sit too, they stare at the carpet, perhaps it tells them something new, perhaps it doesn't. Nurses keep busy, straightening, tidying, checking, doing. They keep watch. She feels safe with them there, the busy nurses, the clever doctors. There are answers here, ways of fixing, measuring, curing. She loves them, but she won't tell them that, that would be mad.

She's not mad, she's just suffering with her nerves. They bring her a cup of tea with a biscuit on the saucer. She has visitors they say. Smiling hard and wide, and pointing to the door. Josie and Gayle, with the little girl, Tamara, stand looking around. They see her and wave. She says to the nurse, make them go away. The nurse don't seem to hear, tells her not to be silly, not to be selfish, so she has to say it again and again, louder and louder till she knows she is definitely saying the words out loud. The little girl is crying.

TAMARA

Her mother is sitting at her patio table, a glass of wine, packet of cigarettes and ash tray in front of her. The girl is opposite, drinking a bottle of beer. They are silent listening to next door's radio through the fence, the children a few doors down shrieking, someone's dog barks. Her mother reaches over the table to her packet of cigarettes and lighter. She lights one, draws hard and tips her head back, blowing smoke in a stream straight up towards the sky.

'You're not going to make trouble are you?'

'Me? Why would I do that? I'm not even going to go to that nasty cow's funeral.'

The girl shifts, the plastic chair wobbling on the uneven paving slabs laid by her mother's ex-boyfriend. They drink and the mother finishes her cigarette and lights another, the smoke circling above them.

'You have to go. It's your mother's funeral.'

'I don't have to do anything after what she's done to me. Calling me a liar, cutting me off. Taking sides with him.'

'Mum, she was an old lady. He's her son.'

'Yeah, and I'm her daughter, but I'm trouble, I'm the slut. I'm the one in the wrong. Not him.'

'He was her carer, she relied on him. If you'd just waited till after she'd died then...'

'So I keep my dirty little secret to keep the peace, right?'

'I don't know.'

'I do know, cos no matter what I'd be a liar to them. No matter what, they've made their mind up. My own mother, turning her back on me.'

'Must be a family trait.' The words only half said drift like the smoke from her mother's cigarette.

'What? What are you talking about?'

She looks away, shaking her head. 'Nothing.'

'No come on, if you've got something to say, say it.'

'Just leave it. We're both upset.'

'Say it, whatever it is. Have the courage of your convictions for once.'

'Well, you never believed me, that's all. You didn't listen when I tried to tell you what happened when I was little. You said I was a liar, that I was attention seeking.' She looks her in the eye, watching her mother's face as she sorts the words into their meanings, wincing as if she has been kicked. Spite fills all her hollow spaces, satisfying an old hunger. Replacing fear. It feels good to hurt her mother finally.

'What do you mean?'

'You used to say I was so difficult, and moody. Did you never ask yourself why? Why all the nightmares and bad behaviour?'

'You're spoilt and selfish. That's why.'

'Right. It's my fault, nothing to do with you or something that happened to me.'

A hand, freckled and heavy, engine grease under the nails, pulls at the elastic of her knickers. They are her Tuesday knickers, but it isn't Tuesday. His knuckles stretch out the letters and the picture of the little girl on the front. His fingers dig and dig but when she wets herself he stops and then uses the same hand to slap her. Dirty little girl. There's more, but she learnt not to feel, not to hear, not to remember. It's not that easy to forget though. It's engrained in us. Encoded in. A dark nucleus in every cell of our body.

'I'm not listening to this. Why are you doing this to me? After all I've sacrificed for you. You'll say anything to hurt me.'

'Oh, come on, Mum.'

'Think you're too good for me now, is that it?'

'No, I don't.'

'You're as bad as her, you're as bad as my mother. I wish you were fucking dead too. Get out. Now. You've been nothing but trouble since the day you were born. Go on, get out.' She leans over the table and hisses in Tamara's face, 'You're dead to me.'

Is there a difference between a secret and a lie? Daughters are so much trouble. Why can't they just keep it to themselves, shoulder the load, carry on. Haven't we all? Kept the peace. Not upset the applecart. Is it really too much to ask?

Why tell your mother the secret that will stop her loving you? What are the words even? She will stop, no matter how carefully you tell her, she will look at you as if you are a stranger, a disgusting, vile, evil stranger. She will believe her sons, her husband, the stranger, because it is easier for her to believe that you are a liar than it is for her to believe such an unspeakable thing. It's not new, or even all that tragic. It's been going on forever, should've kept her mouth shut. Kept her secret. Know her place. We've been warned. But what about unconditional love? That a mother's love knows no limit, no end? Another lie. Sometimes.

CLAIRE

She's hungry. So hungry. She fills herself up with words, food, treats. She sits and eats and reads. Nothing fills her up enough. She wants more and more. She's gone without for so long, why not treat herself now? She deserves it. She's done enough, given enough. They take take take and what has she got left? Nothing. Ungrateful, selfish bastards the lot of 'em. They have complaints, moans, how she didn't give enough, or give too much, how she loved too hard, too little. They don't need her anymore, they've got their own families, their own lives, they don't want her no more. No time for her. Their own mother, their own flesh and blood. But she won't go begging, she won't show 'em how they hurt her. Anyway, they'll soon come running when they need something. Her beautiful boys still visit though. Her sons. Light of her life. All those kids and she only hears from a couple of 'em. Unless they want something. And that Gayle, that lying slut, she will never darken the door again. Liar. Liar. Calling the police, telling filthy stories about her own brother. Her own flesh and blood. Her beautiful boy. Only a disgusting mind could make up a story like that. What did she do to deserve this? Evil bitch that one. Always trouble. Always spiteful and vindictive.

She counts out her tablets, portions them into morning, noon and night, seven days a week. How many of 'em make her better? It don't matter, what a luxury to be cared for by the doctors and nurses. She shifts in her chair, she fills it, spills over the edges, has sores and ulcers that weep and seep and rub. They tell her to lose weight, to make herself better, make herself smaller. But she won't. She won't. She takes up her own space now. No more cutting herself down to fit. She don't need to leave the house anyway, she knows what's out there, the invasion, the strangers, foreigners speaking funny, stealing. Stealing. Her own kids lecture her about her parents, weren't they immigrants? Didn't they come over here from somewhere else? They always know best, they won't let her have her feelings. She's allowed to feel, ain't she? Without someone telling her she was wrong? She ain't leaving the house, she has everything she needs. Everything is here.

All this clutter, Mum, all this clutter, that's what they say about her treasures, her memories, her precious treasures. It's impossible to keep clean, Mum, she knows what that means, that she's filthy, can't keep herself clean and it wasn't so long ago they complained she was too house proud, never sitting still, running herself ragged. How dare they, how dare they? She keeps herself busy. She rolls Den fags, and knits, the excess wool coiled around her little finger erect as a small bird. She reads and eats. Sucks on boiled sweets, drinks tea, dunks biscuits. She reads and reads. She gorges herself. But there is never enough. There will never be enough to fill her emptiness.

ADA

She gives her body over to another man, to his attention, his palpating fingers and penetrating gaze, but this time it is so he can determine her fate, as if her body were an oracle. All these men, with all this knowledge about her physical self. The doctor keeps a professional distance, he is calm and considered, perhaps could even be described as kindly. He removes the stethoscope from his ears and puts it in his pocket, pats her hand and gestures to Robert.

'I'll just speak to your husband for a moment, is that all right?' She nods, quite happy to play the good patient. The two men step outside the bedroom, she hears them mumble, their deep voices a consoling sound. She lies back against the pillows, watching the light move and shift on the wall as the lace curtain dances in the breeze from the open window. She hears the men go downstairs and the front door open and shut. She is aware of footsteps on the gravel drive and a car door slamming shut. The engine as it pulls away. She is in very little pain, she is just so very tired. Her heart is failing, something to do with damage from an earlier illness, something picked up in India perhaps?

She can hear Robert returning, his dull plod up the stairs. He has taken it all very badly. He weeps, professes love, wonders how he will cope without her. He brings her tea, soup, books to read. She barely has the energy to raise her head, but he brings them anyway. He adjusts her pillows, the curtains, the temperature of the room. He conducts the family visits, keeping a strict limit on time and who is allowed to see her.

Sometimes he just sits with her, holding her hand. He complains gently about the hard work of looking after the house, then tells her he doesn't know how she did it for so long, looking after them all. She drifts in and out of sleep. She dreams of Kali, of her sharp teeth, and necklace of skulls. It isn't frightening. Kali lifts her up like a baby, her four arms wrapped around her and she nurses at Kali's breast. When she wakes she longs to go back to sleep and Kali Ma's arms.

With the diagnosis came a decision, but not the one that Robert gently calls putting their affairs in order. They sign a will together and discuss arrangements for the disposal of their bodies and property. She places her jewellery into envelopes and writes the name of the recipients on the front. She leaves Tamara a ruby ring, set in Indian gold. Then she takes the box of letters from her wardrobe and reads every last one. The passionate, ardent letters written to another, earlier version of herself and the ones that young woman wrote back. She feels the kisses, the mouths, the hands, the hard bodies against her all over again. Her loves, her other selves pressed flat on paper.

She makes her decision. She waits for Robert to go out shopping, so that she can burn them. She wraps herself up in her bathrobe and takes the box down to the end of the garden, where Robert burns the autumn leaves and heavy cuttings. A book of matches in her pocket. She makes a pyre of all those words, written in different hands, some curled and formal, some blunt and bold. She thinks of witches and heretics, of sinners burnt to death. Of bodies turning to ash by the Ganges. It is the perfect day for a fire, with only a gentle breeze to fan the flames. It is the perfect day to erase the other truth about her life. She should spare him all this pain and leave him with his memories and his version of their life together, leave him with his image of her, his loving wife.

Instead she replaces the letters in the box and puts it back in its place. She places the key to the lock in an envelope addressed to him. It will seem like an act of revenge, or violence, but she thinks that perhaps it could also be a cleansing, a razing of myths to start something new. He deserves to know the truth;

TAMARA

She is curled on her side in bed, still dressed, the quilt pulled up to her ears. Pav hasn't left: she can hear her cleaning up, scraping plates and loading the dishwasher. She waits for her to leave, to be alone. For the door to bang shut. She is disgusted with herself but too ashamed to get up and face her. This is how easy it is to destroy love and trust. Let your true feelings show and boom, that's it, you're alone. Keep it all in, be a good girl, likeable. Nice or else. The bond is so fragile. Inconstant.

She hears voices, music. Pav has switched the TV on. She turns over on her back and waits. This is not the ending she expected. Not the ending she deserves. There is a gentle knock on the door. 'Tam? You awake?'

'Yeah.' She tries to think of the right words to say. To hold on to her friendship, her love. If she can't perform the right script she will be completely alone. What can she know, with only her short span of experience?

The door opens, spilling light into the room. '*Bake Off* is on, and you know you can't miss it.'

She sits up. 'I'm sorry I shouted. I know I shouldn't have.'

'Don't be daft. C'mon, we're missing it.' Pav holds her hand out.

We gaze at her, our girl, pay close attention, so close that the boundaries blur, smear and fuse – she is us, we, I, you – and what is that but love? Enduring, nestled, bosomed between what was and what will be.

Acknowledgements

Because sometimes the imagined tells the truth better than the facts, this is a work of fiction constructed from ready-made stories. To my grandmothers and all the women in my life, I pay homage. Also, the work and ideas of Mark Fisher were hugely influential in the writing of this novel. His writing remains a constant source of inspiration, involvement and tension.

My love and enormous gratitude are due to Rebekah, Eadaoin, Lindsay and Hetha for reading and rereading and being so patient and generous with comments and suggestions. I'm so lucky to have you in my life.

My thanks also to all at Bluemoose Books: what would we do without you and your passionate commitment to literature? Huge thanks especially to Lin, my inimitable, eagle-eyed and thoughtful editor!

And my beloved family: Joe, Talulah, Raif, Indira and Romi Pearl. You all make everything possible. I love you.